Business Desk Reference

The Supervisor's Handbook

Second Edition

A quick and handy guide for any manager or business owner

The Supervisor's Handbook

Second Edition

A quick and handy guide for any manager or business owner

CAREER PRESS
3 Tice Road, P.O. Box 687
Franklin Lakes, NJ 07417
1-800-CAREER-1
201-848-0310 (NJ and outside U.S.)
Fax: 201-848-1727

THE SUPERVISOR'S HANDBOOK (SECOND EDITION)
A QUICK AND HANDY GUIDE FOR ANY MANAGER OR BUSINESS OWNER

Cover design by Digital Perspectives
Printed in the U.S.A. by Book-mart Press

To order this title, please call toll-free 1-800-CAREER-1
(NJ and Canada: 201-848-0310) to order using VISA or
MasterCard, or for further information on books from
Career Press.

Library of Congress Cataloging-in-Publication Data

The Supervisor's handbook : a quick and handy guide for any
manager or business owner. -- 2nd ed.
    p. cm. -- (Business desk reference)
    ISBN 1-56414-106-3 :
    1. Supervision of employees--Handbooks, manuals, etc. I. Career
Press Inc. II. Series.
    HF5549.17.S86   1993
    658.3'02--dc20   93-26982
                                                                CIP

Table of Contents

Chapter 4   HANDLING EMPLOYMENT ISSUES

Chapter 5   TIME MANAGEMENT

Chapter 6   COMMUNICATION

INTRODUCTION

The effective supervisor or small business owner can multiply the value and benefits he or she contributes to the organization by keeping in mind these considerations covering supervisory responsibility:

1. Remember it is your job to develop and foster the high morale, enthusiasm and esprit de corps of your team.

2. Make it a point to know and understand the objectives of your boss, department and company. Make sure your employees know what their individual objectives are and how they fit into and contribute to the organization's objectives.

3. Keep all members of your team informed about all aspects of their jobs and of the work unit in general.

4. Be familiar with and able to interpret and enforce all company and departmental policies and regulations. To the employee, you are the company.

5. Assign work, overtime, discipline and rewards on an impartial basis that is known and understood by all your team members.

6. Make a continual effort yourself and solicit suggestions from team members on work method improvements.

The Five Most Common Reasons Supervisors/ Small Business Owners Fail

1. *Poor delegation:* As a supervisor or small business owner, you are judged not for the work you do, but for the results you achieve. In order to achieve the greatest results, you must delegate work to other team members. Many supervisors are promoted into positions overseeing work they, themselves, used to do. The temptation to "do it myself" can be almost overwhelming. It's deadly to your career or business. Avoid it at all costs.

2. *Continuing to be a "buddy":* New supervisors promoted from within are especially vulnerable to the temptation to be "one of the gang." Unfortunately, that is usually not the best policy. Because the supervisor must represent other levels of management to the workers and because the supervisor often must make or relay unpopular decisions, the supervisor must strike a balance between being a "buddy" and the practice of the good human relations skills of an effective leader.

3. *Wrong use of authority:* The opposite of the above problem. Unexperienced supervisors or new small business owners sometimes let their new authority go to their heads. No one can be effective for long without the cooperation and support of the team members. One of the surest ways to lose that cooperation and support is to improperly use the authority of your position.

4. *Being a poor role model:* The "don't do as I do, do as I say" school of supervision is long defunct. Always remember that your team looks to you to set the example. This is true regarding your adherence to company policies and rules, your attitude toward upper management and your treatment of others on the work team.

5. *No desire to be a supervisor:* Often people are promoted into supervisory positions they really don't want. Unfortunately, great technical job skills alone don't qualify an individual to be a supervisor. A big ingredient for supervisory success is the desire to be a supervisor. Often this *desire* motivates the person involved to seek ways to develop the additional skills necessary to be a good supervisor — administrative and human relations skills. Small business owners also must have these skills in order to run successful companies. This book will show both supervisors and small business owners how to become better administrators and human resource managers.

EFFECTIVE LEADERSHIP

One of the most sought-after skills for any supervisor is leadership. After all, a supervisor must set a good example for his or her team members to follow. Similarly, a small business owner needs to establish work procedures and provide direction to everyone he or she employs.

How You Can Contribute to Profits

In business today, the bottom line is the bottom line. Everyone plays an important role in making the business profitable.

The supervisor is in an ideal position to contribute to company profitability in two vital ways — cost control and methods improvement. You have direct influence and control over the use of machines and tools, the work methods employed and the attitudes and performance of the workers. Small business owners have the same opportunities for influence and control.

Suggested Cost Control Guidelines and Strategies

1. *Offer incentives to employees for successful cost reduction.* You might let employees share in the savings realized or offer cash awards, time off or other recognition for effective employee efforts.

2. *Cost reduction should be part of "business as usual."* Don't make cost consciousness just a once-a-year effort.

3. *You should set the example.* Remember, as in many other areas, your attitude toward costs sets the tone for the rest of the department.

4. *Set specific objectives.* You must know what current costs are in the target area and set a specific goal of what you want to achieve in savings and by when.

5. *Expect individual accountability.* Employees should be held accountable for the costs under their control.

6. *Be willing to try various approaches.* One technique probably won't work in every area. Match the approach to the problem.

7. *Increase production with the same or fewer resources.*

8. *Streamline work flow.* Irregular work flow with many peaks and valleys is generally not efficient.

9. *Reduce waste.* Minimize unnecessary services, the scrapping of unused materials, idle personnel, work on projects of limited value and idle or under-utilized equipment.

10. *Invest in employee training.* Well-trained, motivated employees are more productive and efficient than those who aren't. Usually, up-front investments in training are returned in increased effectiveness.

11. *Modernize and maintain equipment.* Obsolete or worn equipment should be replaced, upgraded or repaired. Not only does the machine become more efficient, such action generally has a very positive effect on the operator.

Steps to Improving Work Methods

1. *Determine the task to be improved.*

2. *Analyze and question each step in accomplishing the task.* Who does this step? Why is it necessary? Where is it done? How is it done? Why is it done that way?

3. *Develop better methods.* Improvements can generally be made by simplifying, eliminating, combining or changing the sequence of the steps in the job. Usually, only some of the improvements can be applied. Determine which are the best.

4. *Obtain approval from above for implementation of the improvement.* It is usually more persuasive to put your request/suggestion in writing. Your proposal should include a description of the change, how it will work, what it will accomplish, how much it will save in costs or increase in production or quality and what effects it will have on employees.

5. *Implement the improvement and follow up.* Make a special effort to get employee support and involvement in any methods-improvement program. Also, after the improvement has been implemented, be prepared to monitor the change and make minor adjustments.

Improving Your Leadership Efficiency

Many supervisors and small business owners think they will succeed only if they are always on top of everything that goes on under their jurisdiction and direct everything with a firm hand. They don't realize that by doing so they are making life harder for themselves than it needs to be and they are undermining their employees' ability to achieve.

There are many ways to use *indirect* leadership effectively. Here are some tools for eliciting good work from people without peering over their shoulders. How many of these aspects of efficient supervision do you use?

- *An Exciting Vision* — By painting a vivid picture for people of the important outcomes their work will yield, you are giving them something exciting to aim toward, something that will motivate them to invest their best effort without your direct supervision.

- *Self-Confidence* — By reinforcing your employees' beliefs in their own ability to do a great job, you are minimizing their tendency to come to you or to despair when problems arise. Confident people are more eager and willing to do their best at work.

- *Supportiveness* — By being friendly and courteous, by showing people that you are concerned for their well-being, you create a desire on their part to reciprocate — therefore, employees do their best for you even when you are not present.

- *Experienced, Well-Trained People* — By hiring people who know how to do the job and by providing adequate training for people who need to learn new skills, you are assuring that self-direction is available, rather than reliance on direction from you.

- *Group Norms* — When people work together in a group that sets high standards and cares for each other, they tend to pitch in and do their best for the sake of the group. So, forming small, compatible, self-regulating work groups can make supervision easier.

- *Explicit Policies and Procedures* — When work decisions are ambiguous, people tend to look to the supervisor or business owner for direction. When your preferred method of operation is spelled out as clearly as possible (in writing, if appropriate), people feel more confident about the right thing to do and they go about doing it, rather than doing the wrong thing or coming to you for guidance.

- *Ethics* — Many supervisors and small business owners invest a lot of effort making sure that people do what's proper and legal. Employees screened for their ethical standards before being hired, who have a clear, agreed-upon code of honor to follow and who work for someone who sets a good, ethical example can be trusted to do the right thing even without supervision.

- *Satisfying Tasks* — People doing work that they find reasonably pleasant to do require less supervision than people forced to do a job they hate. Checking that jobs under your supervision are designed to be as enjoyable as possible for the people who must do them will relieve you of the need to constantly supervise.

• *Performance Feedback* — When other people, or the work itself, provide employees with information on how well they are doing, they have less need for a supervisor to watch over and evaluate them. Increasing the means whereby employees get feedback from customers or from objective measures of the work they are producing provides sources of assessment other than yourself.

• *Participation* — When people have a voice in making the decisions that will affect their work, they usually are more committed to carrying out those decisions. Therefore, involving employees in determining their own work procedures enlists their efforts toward carrying out those procedures without your constant supervision. Following these methods can make your job as a supervisor or small business owner much easier.

Increasing Your Power

Your job as a supervisor or small business owner is easier when you can get your organization to accomplish the things you believe are necessary when and how you want them. To achieve this goal you need power.

What Are the Sources of Power?

Certain people have more power in an organization than others. Of course, being higher up in the organization or the owner is helpful. But there are many other ways a supervisor can exert power . . . and knowing the sources of power is useful. Power is exerted by:

• Being in a *central role* in the organization. If your unit provides services needed by other people in the organization, you can influence what those people do. They want your cooperation so, in turn, they will cooperate with you.

• *Substitutability* affects power. Doing something no one else can do gives you power. If your functions cannot readily be performed by someone else, people will be hesitant to do anything that will upset you.

- Dealing with *unexpected* situations brings power. You have more power if you can take advantage of unexpected opportunities or problems that arise. If people can look to you for help in critical situations, you can look to them for help when you need it.

- *Information* and *expertise* bring power. The more you know about the organization and its operations, the more people will rely on you and, in turn, provide what you ask.

- *Resources* bring power. Besides information, people also need supplies, equipment and funds to do their jobs. If you are a supplier of any of these things to other people in the organization, they are likely to supply what you need, too.

Increasing Your Power

If you feel you lack clout in your organization, you can take steps to increase it. Building your power base can be done in several ways:

- *Building a Base of Support* — People who have others on their side when they want something done have power. So, developing allies in the organization enhances your influence. People ally with others who help them out, who agree with them on controversial matters and who provide them with information and support when they need it.

- *Associate with Influential People* — Some people in your organization have more power than others — these are the allies to cultivate. They can be identified by their titles and by their possession of the kinds of power listed above. Get to know them and be sure that they know about you and the work you do. Having a "sponsor" or "mentor" among the more powerful people in your organization can be very helpful throughout your career.

- *Image-Building* — People often judge others' power on the basis of their general appearance and manner. Some people simply look and act as if they have a great deal of power and so others treat them as if they do. A powerful image is developed through dress — more formal attire, for example, usually signals a powerful position. A powerful image is also developed through communication style — people who sound as if they know what they are doing appear more powerful than people who seem unsure of themselves, hesitant or deferential.

- *Create Obligation to Reciprocate* — People feel an inherent desire to reciprocate when someone does a favor for them. The barter system is built into human nature and into organizational life. Do things for others and they will be very willing to do things for you. And don't hesitate to ask people to pay back a favor. People really are more comfortable reciprocating one good turn with another than remaining indebted to someone.

How to Make Better Decisions

Neither making snap decisions nor always having to "sleep on it" is the best approach to the time factor involved in making a decision. Make your decisions based upon the circumstance and the time available. Within the realm of practicality, give yourself enough time to take the following decision-making steps.

1. *Define the problem.* Be careful not to confuse symptoms of the problem with the real problem.

2. *Identify the options.* Try to get at least four alternatives. Since you may be too close to the situation, seek others' input.

3. *Gather the facts.* In order to evaluate your options, you must gather the facts about the ramifications of choosing each option. List both the pros and cons of each option.

4. *Evaluate the options.* Usually this will include a comparison of costs, time required to implement and the expected end result of each option.

5. *Choose and put into effect.* Key, and often neglected, aspects of implementing decisions are to communicate the decision to the affected parties, outline why the decision was made, why the particular option was picked, what actions are required on their part and what beneficial results are expected.

Decision Pitfalls to Avoid

1. *Deciding alone.* There are many benefits to consulting with others on a decision: gaining different perspectives, more resources to draw upon and more commitment to the decision by those consulted.

2. *Every decision a major decision?* Not every decision requires a lengthy decision-making process. Don't get bogged down with minor problems. If they're minor, make a reasonable decision and move on.

3. *"The last time I was wrong was when I thought I made a mistake."* No one is always right. If you've made a bad decision, admit it and get started on fixing it. Remember—it's impossible to force a bad decision into being a good one.

4. *"Boy! I sure wish I hadn't."* Just the opposite of Pitfall #3. Because no one can be right all the time, don't waste your energy regretting bad decisions. Get on to current issues.

5. *Failing to use past precedent.* Maybe the same problem has come up before and been effectively solved. Perhaps, if it has come up enough, there is a company policy that covers it.

The Importance of Developing Plans

All successful companies of any size have solid, working business plans in place. While a supervisor may play a part in developing the plans for his or her particular work group, the small business owner usually bears the responsibility for drawing up the entire plan for his or her company. Whatever your position, it's important for you to understand the basics of building a strategic business plan.

Generally, most businesses do their strategic business planning on a yearly basis. Once a plan has been developed, it can be reviewed, revised and refocused annually as needed. There are six steps involved in strategic business planning.

The Strategic Business Planning Process

1. *Write a mission statement.* Keep the statement as short and to-the-point as possible so employees understand and remember it.

2. *Make a situational analysis of the business, including both internal and external assessments.* The internal assessment examines the history of the business in terms of financial information, operational information, business facilities, products and services, market share, customer profiles, marketing efforts and human resources issues. The external assessment looks at how external factors have affected business in the past and how they may affect business in the future. External assessment factors include legislation, government regulations, environmental and safety laws, the economy, taxes, real estate values, unemployment rates, consumer demographics, technological advancements and, most importantly, competing businesses.

3. *Identify the business' strengths, weaknesses, opportunities and threats.* To complete this part of the strategic plan, consider asking supervisors and other key employees to take part in a brainstorming session and make actual lists.

4. *Identify four or five critical issues that impact business.* These are usually one- or two-word issues such as *profitability, product or service quality, business development, training* and *employee relations.* While many more probably could be named, it's better to focus on a few issues which can be targeted for improvement during the plan year.

5. *State the desired position of the business in a given time frame.* In this portion of the strategic plan refer back to each of the critical issues identified and ask, "Where do I want my business to be in

terms of profitability in three years?" By answering that question, measurable goals can be set.

6. *Devise strategies.* Refer again to each of the critical issues and the goals set for them in step five. This time the question is, "What can we do to insure that our goals are met?" Using the example of profitability, possible answers may be cutting costs and increasing sales. Then ask, "How are we going to achieve our goals?" The specific answers to this question become the basis for the business operational plan. For example, to achieve profitability, you might decide to find alternative suppliers in order to cut costs and to identify potential new customers in order to increase sales.

The Five W's and an H for Developing Plans

Whether you're a small business owner or a supervisor, it's important to involve all employees in the strategic planning process. Assign them each responsibilities for attaining business goals and make sure they understand the direction in which the business is headed. This empowers employees to do their best work and ultimately makes the business more successful.

Here are some questions to consider when involving employees in the strategic planning process.

1. *What must be done?* What actions must be taken to reach the objective?

2. *Why must it be done?* Is the investment of resources justified?

3. *When should it be done?* Dates, time frames and deadlines should be selected and coordinated.

4. *Who should do it?* Appropriate personnel must be selected.

5. *Where should it be done?* Related to the previous question. Where will the appropriate people and equipment be located?

6. *How should it be done?* What are the ways and means? Can current methods be used or should new ones be developed?

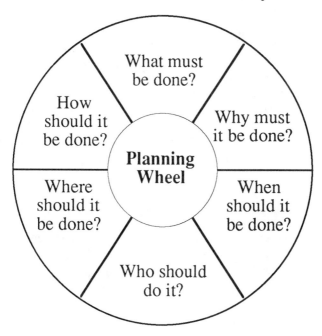

How to Set Objectives

For your business objectives to have the best chance for success, they should have these characteristics:

1. *Objectives should be specific and measurable.* For example: "To increase sales by 15 percent by June 1st," not just, "To increase sales."

2. *Objective-setting should include those responsible for achieving the objective.* Workers are more committed to the successful attainment of goals they help create.

3. *Objectives should be challenging but attainable.* Objectives recognized as impossible are extremely de-motivating to workers. On the other hand, goals that require workers to really "stretch" but are attainable can be very motivating. People receive satisfaction from reaching goals and, consequently, are that much more motivated to reach for the next one.

4. *Objectives should be regularly reviewed and updated.* Going after outdated objectives is a waste of time and people. The validity of objectives should be reviewed periodically.

5. *Objectives should be ranked.* At any given time, your work team will be pursuing several objectives. Obviously, some will be of much greater importance than others. Make sure your people are aware of the relative importance of the objectives so they can allocate their time and resources accordingly.

Changing Established Work Patterns

Conditions within and outside most organizations are constantly changing. It follows, therefore, that the way work is organized and accomplished must change periodically to cope with changing conditions. Most people agree with Rosabeth Moss Kanter that the best supervisors now are "change masters." Small business owners often must initiate change and lead the way for others to follow.

You may develop a plan or be instructed by higher-ups to change some equipment, work methods, rules, control practices, job design, lines of communication or authority or any other aspect of your work area. The idea may be good, but implementing it often isn't easy — people tend to resist change. To cope with resistance we have to understand why it occurs and how it can be overcome.

Why Do People Resist Change?

Here are the most common reasons:

1. *Self-Interest* — People fear that change will cause them to lose something they once had. For example, when a corporate president decided to create a new vice presidency for product development, the existing vice presidents for manufacturing and marketing resisted because they feared losing their existing right to approve or veto new product decisions.

2. *Misunderstanding and Lack of Trust* — A change starts as a vision in the mind of its sponsor. If people don't trust that individual, they will suspect that he or she has hidden and harmful motives for proposing the change. For example, a union opposed a company's proposal of flexible scheduling (flextime) because they didn't trust the personnel manager who suggested it.

3. *Different Assessments* — When people view a problem from different perspectives, they will perceive different causes and cures for it. Therefore, they may see a change as tackling the wrong cause and proposing a fruitless solution. For example, sanitation department employees felt their pick-up delays were due to equipment breakdowns so they resented the city replacing their supervisor — they felt the planned change was inappropriate.

4. *Low Tolerance for Change* — People sometimes resist change because they fear they will be unable to handle the new conditions competently. They also may resist breaking up comfortable social relations with co-workers. For example, individuals have turned down transfers and promotions because they weren't sure they could handle being supervisors and they didn't want to give up the friendships with co-workers that had developed over the years.

How Is Resistance to Change Overcome?

Five major ways can be used to deal with resistance to change. Each is especially appropriate when certain conditions exist.

When:	*Use this method:*
Employees poorly understand or have little or inaccurate information about the problem.	Provide, in advance, as much information as possible about the change and your reasons for it.
You don't have all the information needed to design the change and where others have considerable power to resist.	Allow the people who will be affected by the change to participate in deciding what needs to be done and how to implement the changes.
People are resisting because they feel put out and inconvenienced by having to change from familiar to new circumstances.	Help people adjust to the new conditions by making the change as comfortable as possible.
Someone (or a group) clearly will lose out in a change, and they have power to resist.	Negotiate with them so they feel somewhat compensated for what is to be lost due to change.
Speed is essential, and you have considerable power to enforce your will.	Announce and enforce the change with certainty and firmness.

These methods usually are used in combination and they are successful when employed with realistic awareness of the situation in which change is to occur.

Change: Cherished Social Arrangements

Efforts to change things in an organization can flop if they alter "cherished social arrangements." For example, executives at an automobile plant proposed to stagger the stopping and starting times of work for different departments. Their intention was to decrease traffic congestion when workers arrived and left at the same time every morning and evening.

They didn't expect resistance to this evidently helpful plan. But the workers objected vehemently. Many had been driving to work together in car-pools for 10 years or more and these groups often were made up of people from different departments. The staggered-time proposal, aimed at relieving traffic congestion, lost out because it threatened long-standing personal relationships.

The most effective business leaders today include their employees in their business decisions whenever possible. Their efforts foster the emergence of a team in which all members work together for the good of the business.

2

THE IMPORTANCE OF TEAMWORK

So how do you build a team that's committed to helping your company succeed? It's a process that takes time and that must be woven into every element of your business day.

Running Efficient Meetings

As a supervisor or small business owner, you probably have to pull your people together from time to time for meetings — at which you share information and discuss with them the issues you must resolve together. Meetings take a lot of time and are often frustrating. It is awkward for more than two or three people to coordinate their conversations and ideas into a satisfying whole — as a result, people usually dread meetings.

As a team leader, you can do several things to be sure that your meetings function as efficiently as possible. How many of these practices do you regularly employ?

- *Consider beforehand whether a meeting actually is necessary.* Often, a scheduled meeting can be replaced with a phone call, a personal visit to someone's work site or a memo.

- *Consider who should attend the meeting.* Who must be present and who need not be? For every decision, some people should participate in making it, some people should be consulted before a final decision is made and others should be informed about tentative decisions before they are made public. Usually, the latter two groups need not be present at the meeting. People with an ambiguous role (vis-a-vis the meeting's business) should be given the opportunity to decide for themselves about attending.

- *Send out an agenda in advance.* A preview of the meeting ought to go out a few days ahead of time so everyone knows what to expect and can make the necessary preparations. The agenda should include these items:

  1. What business the meeting will address.

  2. What the group will do and accomplish regarding each item. For example, hear a report, share viewpoints informally and/or make a decision.

  3. How much time participants should allocate for the entire meeting.

  4. Approximately how much time will be given to each item on the agenda. When a schedule of meeting episodes is available, people can attend for just the portion of the meeting that is of greatest interest to them and they need not sit through a lot of irrelevant discussion.

  5. How participants should prepare for the meeting.

  6. What material participants should bring to the meeting.

- *Always start the meeting at precisely the scheduled time.* By consistently doing this, you will avoid a lot of wasted time.

- *Have someone else keep a running account of the minutes* of the meeting by writing them on a large flipchart or overhead projector in front of the group. When announcements, main points and decisions are on public display throughout the meeting, the likelihood of misunderstanding and unnecessary repetition is reduced. For example, when people repeat ideas already expressed, you can point to the recorded information and say, "That's already up there."

- *When you have a strong opinion on a topic, ask someone else to take over chairing the meeting.* This allows you to state your opinion on a controversial topic without seeming to misuse your authority as leader of the group. It shows that you are willing to entertain other viewpoints while you do not intend to stifle or disguise your own. Also, letting other people preside, especially individuals who tend to oppose you, gives them a chance to see how difficult being neutral can be.

Are You a Participant in a Wasteful Meeting?

What can you do when you are a participant in meetings that run too long and accomplish very little?

1. *Ask for time limits.* When you are told about the meeting, ask the leader how long it is expected to last. In the event that the meeting runs overtime, you will have a valid excuse for leaving (to keep another appointment you have set up on the basis of the time limit you had been told) or for calling for the meeting to end.

2. *Ask for a statement of contributions.* Ask the meeting leader what the purpose of the meeting is and whether any planning or preparation will be required of those attending. Questions of this type will motivate the leader to specify the purpose of the meeting and its agenda and to clarify what needs to be done ahead of time for the meeting to achieve its goals.

3. *Provide leadership functions.* Fill in the leadership actions that are being omitted yourself, such as offering to prepare an agenda, suggesting that a specific proposal be made when the group is meandering abstractly or calling for a straw vote when you think people are arguing over a point on which you believe most group members actually agree.

4. *Don't attend the meeting.* It may cost you less to deal with that absence than to sit and stew and watch your time fly by.

Forming and Leading Quality Circles

Many American organizations are following the lead of Japanese corporations and creating "quality circles" in the workplace. A quality circle is a group of people who work together and who also hold periodic meetings to discuss how they can solve problems and improve the quality and efficiency of their shared efforts.

Usually, a quality circle contains no more than 12 people and meets once a week on company time. The group's supervisor usually meets with them and sometimes a discussion facilitator as well. Some quality circles choose someone other than the supervisor to serve as the discussion leader — they rotate that role so the group operates as democratically as possible.

If quality circle members and their leader are well-trained for their roles in the group, they can make valuable contributions to the organization's productivity. For example, one quality circle in a large manufacturing firm recently found that it had to wait an average of 30 minutes per day for a cart on which to ship its finished products to the quality control area. The cost of an additional cart was $100. The circle recommended buying a new cart and showed, through its calculations, that the firm would recover the investment in less than 10 working days. This was a small matter, but multiply savings of this kind many times and you can see that quality circles bring increases in quality, economy and morale.

You may be called upon to act as a quality circle leader or you may want to take the initiative to create one. If so, you need to know how they operate and how they are led.

Quality Circles Are Based on Two Major Principles:

1. People who carry out or have first-hand knowledge about a task know best what problems exist and how to solve them.

2. People are more committed to implementing solutions that they, themselves, devise and agree upon.

   So the quality circle leader must help the group to identify the problems that exist in his or her unit and to decide upon ways to correct them.

Most Quality Circle Sessions Have Several Standard Components:

1. At the beginning of the meeting, the previous issues considered by the group are summarized. The members need to know that the decisions made at earlier meetings are being acted upon so they feel that their time and effort actually have been making a difference. They also need to know specific performance results of past actions they have taken so both they and the company learn the extent to which changes instituted from their recommendations have positively affected the company.

2. The group then identifies new problems that need consideration. These are listed, and the most important or urgent one is selected by the group for concentrated attention.

3. The group decides what information is needed to fully understand the problem at hand. They may have to devise a record-keeping system for the upcoming week to learn just how frequently the problem arises or how costly it is. Or, they may need to invite someone from outside the group to discuss problems that come from or subsequently affect other units.

4. When essential information is gathered, possible solutions are thrown out by group members. After alternative solutions are listed, the group decides upon criteria to use in identifying the best way to handle the problem. Finally, they select the solution that seems most likely to result in improving their performance and/or making work more satisfying for them.

5. The supervisor usually agrees to present the proposed solution to higher-ups who need to be kept informed and/or who must approve the solutions.

    When these procedures are followed consistently and skillfully, quality circles are a valued and cost-effective use of employees' time.

Improving Relationships Among Groups

Groups working for the same organization often act as if they were with competing companies. You may find that the supervisor and members of another group are obstructing, rather than helping, your group do its job. As a small business owner or supervisor, you may need to diffuse conflict among groups. If this happens, it will be helpful for you to know why groups tend to conflict and how you can reconcile their differences.

Reasons for Inter-Group Conflict

What causes groups to compete?

- *Interdependency* — When groups depend on each other to get their work done, they get frustrated when things go wrong and tend to blame the other group for the problems that exist.

- *Limited resources* — When groups don't have enough equipment or material to get their work done, competition among them for those scarce resources becomes likely.

- *Independent rewards* — When groups are rewarded only on the basis of their own work, the organization is reinforcing them for struggling against each other rather than for cooperating.

- *Different goals* — When groups' goals differ — for example, one group (such as sales) is most concerned with the amount of business generated and another group (such as manufacturing) wants to make only flawless products — their inharmonious goals will generate conflict.

- *Different time periods* — When one group is concerned with meeting short-term deadlines and another group pays more attention to long-range achievements, they are each likely to see the other as ignoring or obstructing their own efforts.

- *Status incongruity* — When one group gets more credit or rewards for its work than another group, resentment between them will grow.

- *Different perceptions* — When one group gets partial and distorted information about what another group does, it will often misunderstand and misjudge the other group's actions.

Remember: Knowing what causes inter-group conflict is the first step in alleviating it.

Solutions for Inter-Group Conflict

When your group and other groups in your organization begin to develop negative stereotypes about each other and feel pleased when the other groups fail, you need to intervene. How can you rebuild harmony and cooperation? By decreasing competition:

Decreasing Competition between Two Groups — People who feel they are working on the same side of the line are less likely to feel competitive. Unity is built by:

1. *Emphasizing the common enemy* — Opposing groups unite when they recognize that they are facing a threat bigger than each other. When employees realize that they face the danger of losing contracts to a competing company or of losing their jobs altogether, they are motivated to rally together and to compromise their differences — which usually seem minor in the big picture.

2. *Increasing cooperative rewards* — When management provides recognition to both groups equally and when it rewards each group somewhat on the basis of how well it meshes its work with the work of the other group, both groups are encouraged to cooperate.

3. *Task force meetings* — Representatives from each group should meet periodically to plan and to discuss progress made on specific projects involving the two groups.

4. *Reducing inter-group distance* — Arrangements are made for groups that are interdependent to work as nearby each other as possible so members can readily communicate during work breaks and can reach each other immediately when problems arise.

Every opportunity taken to emphasize that the two groups have more to gain by cooperating than by competing and to help them get to know each other well helps in resolving inter-group conflict.

How to Build Teamwork

In order for a group of people to attain their maximum potential as a team, these conditions must be met:

1. The group must have a common goal.

2. The members must have a mutual trust for one another.

3. Each member must have a thorough understanding and acceptance of the system of rewards, discipline and work sharing. This system must be clearly articulated and embraced by upper management or the small business owner.

The Four Steps to Building a Team

1. *The supervisor must see to it that the work environment is (and is perceived by the team members as) fair, reasonable and friendly.* Unfortunately, the supervisor cannot do this alone. All levels of management, including the business owner, have an impact. But, if the supervisor doesn't actively see that this environment is established with the work unit, all the efforts of upper management will be to no avail.

2. *The supervisor must demonstrate an ability to see things from the worker's point of view.* Not from the negative attitude of, "It's us against upper management," but from the perspective that the supervisor has the empathy to understand the issues from the employees' side of things.

3. *The supervisor must strive to gain acceptance as the group's leader.* While the supervisor has formal authority that has been delegated down from upper management levels, his or her effectiveness will be greatly enhanced by the willing support of the team members.

4. *Encouraging employee contribution to working out problems, participating in decision-making and so forth also boosts commitment and team spirit.* Similarly, team members also value being kept up-to-date about things that will affect them, the work unit or the company.

Five Steps to Increased Team Productivity

1. *Set a specific, attainable improvement goal.* Improvement should first be sought in those areas where volume or quality of work is below par. Compare this with what the supervisor and team members believe should be accomplished. Mutual agreement is reached on where to start. There should also be general agreement on how the improvement will be accomplished.

2. *Remove the roadblocks to success.* Make a list of the obstacles blocking progress toward the goal. All team members should participate in determining ways to remove or work around the obstacles.

3. *Make certain all team members are aware of and committed to the accomplishment of sought-after goals.* Everyone must know what is going to be done, how it is going to be done and why it is important to them.

4. *Groom the team.* Each team member's contribution is important to the accomplishment of the unit's objectives. Recognizing this fact, assess each member's abilities. Give extra training or instruction to those who need it. If necessary, transfer the employee to a position where he or she can contribute appropriately.

5. *Keep them informed.* A winning team always wants to know the score. Information on how, when, why and where the team members are in relation to achieving their goals has positive effects. It tells them where the team stands and gives them recognition for what they are doing. This information should be frequent and complete.

Teamwork

Share this paragraph with team members who believe that "doing your own thing" is all that matters.

My supervisxr txld me that teamwxrk depends xn the perfxrmance xf every single persxn xn the team. I ignxred that idea until my supervisxr shxwed hxw the xffice typewriter perfxrms when just xne single key is xut xf xrder. All the xther keys xn xur typewriter wxrk just fine except xne, but that xne destrxys the effectiveness xf the typewriter. Nxw I knxw that even thxugh I am xnly xne persxn, I am needed if the team is tx wxrk as a successful team shxuld.

Managing Conflict

Conflict between people usually follows a series of stages:

1. People want something but run into someone who *disagrees* with them or *obstructs* their progress.

2. Both parties feel *frustrated* because they can't do or get what they want.

3. They explain their frustration by *blaming* each other.

4. They feel angry and *do* or *say* things based on how they have come to interpret what happened.

5. Both parties *react,* and the conflict escalates.

6. Someone perceives that the conflict could get out of hand and initiates a way to *manage* it. Here's where conflict management skills are needed. Several techniques may be used.

Alternatives for Managing Conflict

Kenneth Thompson identified five common methods for managing a conflict situation:

1. Being *dominant* or *forceful*

2. *Giving in* or *accommodating*

3. Creating a *trade-off* or *compromise*

4. *Avoiding* or *postponing* the conflict

5. *Collaborating* for a *"win-win," integrative solution*

Thompson then asked 28 chief executive officers of companies which approach they used. He found that they used all five, but each under different circumstances. Following are the methods and when to use them. When a conflict arises, use the approach that best fits the situation.

(Handbook of Industrial and Organizational Psychology, published by Rand McNally)

1. Insist upon your preference — be *dominating* and *forceful:*

   • In an emergency when quick, decisive action is vital.

   • On important issues — when unpopular actions need implementing, when cutting costs, or when enforcing strict rules or disciplinary measures.

   • On issues vital to the organization's welfare when you are very sure that you're right.

   • With people who take advantage of others' consideration.

2. *Giving in* and *accommodating* the other person:

   • When you may be wrong, to give way to a better position or to show how reasonable you are.

   • When issues are much more important to others than to you to satisfy them and to maintain cooperation.

   • To build up social credit so you can request reciprocation in the future.

   • To minimize loss when you are out-matched and losing.

   • When harmony and goodwill are especially important.

   • To help team members grow by permitting them to go ahead and make a mistake and learn from it.

3. Create a *trade-off* or suggest a mutual *compromise*:

   • When your opponent has equal power and you both are committed to mutually exclusive goals.

   • To achieve temporary settlements to complex issues.

   • To arrive at an expedient solution when you're under time pressure.

   • When your goal is important but not worth the effort of being more assertive with a resistant person.

4. Just *avoid* or *postpone* a conflict:

   • When an issue is trivial or more important issues are pressing.

   • When you see no chance of things going your way.

   • When potential disruption outweighs the benefits of pursuing the matter.

   • To let people cool down and gain perspective.

   • When someone else is in a better position to resolve the conflict.

   • When the issue is minor or symptomatic of deeper problems.

5. Generally, the best method for managing conflict is to *collaborate*, to create a *"win-win"* or an *integrative solution* that satisfies both parties:

   • When both sets of concerns are too important to be compromised.
   • To merge insights of people with different perspectives.

   • To gain long-term commitment by reaching genuine consensus among everyone involved.

   • When feelings that have built up during the conflict need to be worked through before a satisfactory agreement can be reached.

Building a successful and effective working team is not without its challenges and failures, but the effort will reap many rewards for your company.

GETTING THE MOST FROM YOUR EMPLOYEES

It is said that the CEO of a large organization used to take all candidates for supervisory positions on a walk across the landscaped grounds of his company's headquarters. He always stopped with them at a fish pond. He asked them to look into the pond and tell him what they saw.

When asked why he did this, the CEO replied, "What they report seeing tells me about their ability to be supervisors. I am more willing to hire those who tell me they see the fish swimming around. Those who report seeing their image mirrored in the water are too much in love with their own egos. I don't want them working for me."

The same story could be told about a small business owner who wants to make sure that he or she hires the best people to help run the company.

Having the right mix of people is essential for any successful business. As a small business owner or supervisor, there are several things you can do to ensure that you get the most from your employees.

How to Motivate People

Perhaps you've got employees who don't seem to be putting forth their best efforts. What can you do to get those employees to do their utmost? Consider, of course, whether they are getting the basics — fair pay, decent working conditions and job security. But what if they are getting those essentials and are still not motivated? What secrets of motivating people go beyond what's obvious?

Secret #1: Individual Differences

People are motivated by different things. What one person wants, another person may think is unimportant.

Besides pay and promotions, what makes *you* work hard? Probably some of the things on the list below are really important to you while others may not be.

Do this exercise — rate each item as:

VI — Very Important
I — Important
NI — Not Important

_____ *Recognition* — you know people appreciate what you do.

_____ *Responsibility* — you know it's your job to do; the credit or blame will fall on your shoulders.

_____ *Enjoying the work* — you like your job.

_____ *Good co-workers* — you like the people you work with and want to do well for their sake.

_____ *Doing a good job* — you feel satisfied only when the work you do turns out well.

_____ *Status* — you feel important at work and people look up to you.

_____ *Challenge* — your job calls for your full attention and skillfulness.

_____ *Growth* — your work gives you opportunities to learn new things.

Next, when talking to people who aren't fully motivated, give them this checklist. Or use the list when discussing with these individuals what really matters to them about their work.

You're likely to find that their preferences differ from yours. When you learn what their "hot buttons" are, you'll know how to motivate them!

Secret #2: Expecting to Succeed, Expecting to Fail

The best motivation system in the world won't work unless people expect to succeed within it. Some people aren't motivated by the usual incentives because they have negative expectations about two things. These questions will elicit their expectations:

1. Will you be able to do what's wanted? Will your efforts produce the kind of performance the organization expects?

    Your employees must feel the answer is "yes" to this question or else putting forth their full effort at work will seem pointless — they will expect to fail, so they won't really try.

2. Will improving your performance bring the rewards you want? Does hard work around here actually lead to getting more of what motivates you?

    Your employees must also feel the answer is "yes" to this question. Otherwise, they will feel that putting forth more effort won't make much difference.

If you are motivated at work, chances are that your answers to both sets of questions are "yes."

Ask these crucial expectation questions of unmotivated workers. Chances are their answers to one or both will be "no."

If so, you must work on changing their expectations, either of themselves or of your organization.

Seeing Results

People feel motivated and proud when they believe they are doing meaningful work. Too often, however, they are not present when what they produce ultimately is put to use. When such a situation exists, supervisors and small business owners should try to make it possible for employees to see the fruits of their labor.

Richard Boschetto is vice president of Smith Construction Products in Los Angeles, which has a job shop that employs 15 to 30 people in manufacturing metal wall, roof and floor systems. Some of the larger projects that have used their services are the UNLV sports arena in Las Vegas, the MGM in Reno and the Hyatt Hotel in Long Beach. But the hourly employees see only the pieces of each structure that they work on in the shop.

When Boschetto started with the company, this shop was riddled with labor problems. He instituted many reforms to enhance motivation. One activity was particularly effective.

Boschetto describes it this way:

"When we finished some of our large jobs in the Los Angeles area, I rented a bus at the noon hour — the first shift works from 6 a.m. to 2:30 p.m. — and boarded the 20-plus hourly workers and the four management personnel for a trip to three job sites in the area. The reaction when these workers saw the end result of their efforts was 'Wow!' "

Give your staff members a chance to see the meaningful results of their efforts, and they will grow in enthusiasm and the desire to do a job they can feel proud of.

Involving Families

At RMI, a U.S. Steel plant making titanium metal in Niles, Ohio, employee morale is boosted through family involvement.

Management believes that families are interested in where their member(s) works. They use two methods to keep families informed:

1. The company publication, *Spirit*, is mailed to the employees' homes.

2. Families are specifically invited to plant open houses. At these open houses, exhibits are displayed that describe how the company's products are used now and how they might be used in the future. Tour guides are both union and salaried personnel. When the workers on the floor explain to their families what they actually do,

their pride and involvement with their company grow.

RMI also has made available to employees and their families some unused land near the Niles facility for "Victory Gardens." Employees can voluntarily sign up for a garden plot. They are responsible for farming and maintaining the plot while RMI does the plowing.

Rewards

At IBM, outstanding achievement is encouraged by means of rewards. Money is the prize generally won. The amount need not be exorbitant.

One of IBM's most popular and effective rewards, for example, is called a "Dinner for Two."

Any manager, without further approval, is allowed to tell an employee, "You've done a good job on this; take your spouse out to dinner. Here's a check for $100."

This modest reward, granted with no further bureaucratic procedure, pays off handsomely in increased motivation — for both the givers and receivers of the rewards.

Motivation

Frequent Salary Increments

The possibility of an annual or semi-annual raise spurs employees to greater effort, so receiving raises even more often than that can help keep motivation at a high pitch all year long.

Michael Dunaway, CEO of Psicor, Inc., provides his employees a pay increase with each salary check — every two weeks.

Psicor, which has fewer than 150 employees, provides equipment and personnel to assist in open-heart surgery. Consequently, its staff must be productive and dedicated. Dunaway wants them to feel appreciated day after day, and he thinks a year is a long time to wait between raises.

So, although there isn't actually much increased expense, the program boosts morale by communicating to the staff that the company cares enough to recognize good work continuously.

Praising and Rewarding People Effectively

People work for the rewards their efforts will bring. Supervisors and small business owners who effectively provide desired outcomes for their employees will gain continued and additional effort from them. Those who shortchange their employees or administer rewards unfairly will be demotivating. Handling rewards involves knowing what people find rewarding and providing those rewards effectively.

What Do Employees Want?

For every job there are two kinds of rewards: internal and external.

Internal rewards come from doing the job itself. Jobs are inherently rewarding when:

- They involve skills workers enjoy using.

- They involve doing tasks from beginning to end. (Workers have a sense of completion and satisfaction.)

- Workers have reason to believe that they have done a good job — and therefore feel worthwhile.

- Workers learn new things as they work.

Rewarding your workers in these ways requires you to establish for them inherently gratifying tasks to perform. Every time you make life at work more satisfying for your employees, you are increasing the rewards they reap from doing their jobs well — *and* you make them want to continue to do so.

External rewards come after doing a good job. The external kinds of rewards that motivate are:

- Pay and bonuses

- Promotions

- Time off, vacations, benefits

- Status indicators such as a title or a nice office

- Recognition and praise

When employees see, from the organization's formal policies and from the experience of people around them, that good work and only good work — not ordinary or poor work — yields the external rewards, these rewards motivate and serve as an incentive for them to improve.

Effective Praising

People want to know how they are doing and they want to know that their efforts make a difference to their supervisors and small business owners. Therefore, good supervisors make a consistent effort to "catch their people doing something right."

Blanchard and Johnson, in their book, *The One-Minute Manager*, provide the following suggestions for effective praising:

- Let your employees know in advance that you will often tell them how they are doing by giving them feedback on their work performance.

- When you learn that someone has done a good job, praise that person as soon afterward as possible. Don't wait for the annual performance review to do so.

- Be very specific about what action pleased you. Don't rely on general affirmations of the person.

- Include in your praising how good you, yourself, feel about what they did right. Also mention the helpful impact his or her actions have on the organization and on the other people who work there.

- Don't rush your praising. Stop for a moment of silence to let the employee really feel that you genuinely mean what you're saying.

- Encourage the individual to continue doing more of the same.

- When appropriate, shake hands or touch the person in a way that makes it clear how much you support his or her success in the organization.

People thrive on these "strokes" from their supervisors. Provide them generously and both you and your employees will be more satisfied and energized at work.

Structuring People's Jobs

Organizing and dividing up the work in your unit or small business is often left up to you. Since you will be deciding who does what, remember that how an individual's job is structured can greatly affect his or her satisfaction and productivity at work.

When designing a group's job responsibilities, you have two basic variables to work with:

1. *Range* — how many different things each person is asked to do.

2. *Depth* — how much discretion people will have to do things as they wish

People have different preferences regarding these two factors. Some people like simple jobs where they have few responsibilities; others like varied work with a lot of decision-making power. Give people less variety and authority than they prefer and they become bored and restless; give them too much and they become confused and anxious. People work best when their tolerance for range and depth match the work they do. Part of your job as a supervisor or small business owner is to find the ideal balance between the two extremes for each of your employees.

Enriching Jobs

Bright, capable people — those you want to retain in your unit or company — generally prefer greater range and depth. They want to feel that they are doing something important and using their skills fully. Effective supervisors and small business owners use a variety of methods to enrich jobs so that they challenge their outstanding employees. Consider how well you are structuring the jobs you supervise so that they include these factors:

- *Variety of Tasks* — Instead of doing a few things repeatedly, work is clustered so that each person performs a number of different operations.

- *Autonomy* — Instead of following detailed rules and regulations, people have some authority to plan and carry out their work as they think best.

- *Task Identity* — Instead of performing only a small, anonymous part of a large project, people do entire projects on their own so they feel that the final product is in some sense theirs.

- *Feedback* — Instead of laboring away with little sense of how well they are doing, people are given frequent feedback on how much they are accomplishing and how well they are doing their work.

- *Dealing With Clients* — Instead of completely separating the people who do the "inside" and the "outside" work in an organization, everyone is given some contact with the customers or clients who eventually make use of or benefit from the work they do.

- *Friendship Opportunities* — Instead of isolating workers from each other or making interaction at work very formal and businesslike, people are encouraged to form warm, personal bonds with others at work so they develop long-lasting loyalties to each other and to the organization.

- *New Learning* — Instead of training employees only at the start of their employment and having them do the same things until they are promoted, people are frequently taught new procedures so that they feel they are growing personally and expanding their expertise on the job.

- *Scheduling* — Instead of having everyone come in, work and leave at the same time set by the organization, employees are given leeway in deciding their work schedules (flex-time) and rate of productivity.

- *Participating in Decision-Making* — Instead of telling employees what the company plans to do, they are given information about the situations under review and invited to input information and ideas into the decision-making process.

- *Job Rotation* — Instead of people being stuck doing the things they customarily do, they are given opportunities to switch roles with other staff members so they learn more about the other parts of the organization and their functions.

Job-Sharing — Another Option for Job Enrichment

Consider this:

If there is an aspect of your job that you don't enjoy or do as well as someone else at work, you should consider the possibility of sharing that function with a co-worker.

This strategy is akin to the recent trend toward job-sharing between husbands and wives who are parents of small children and share jobs by working half-time each.

The same principle can be applied with parts of a job that are less attractive to some people than to others. Some people are better with figures, some are better at public speaking, some are better organized, some are more creative. If you work side-by-side with someone whose skills complement yours, you might consider partial job-sharing by bartering job functions — "I'll help draft your annual report if you'll help plan this marketing campaign."

Hiring New Employees

Once you've established a successful working team, you need to take extra care when adding new members. That's especially true for small businesses. Because the staff is smaller, each and every employee in a small business plays a bigger part in how well the business does.

Supervisors in larger companies often play an important role in hiring new employees. While they may not make the final decision, supervisors often narrow the list of finalists for the job and provide valuable input.

The Seven-Step Interview Process

Learning good interviewing techniques will help you make the right hiring decisions. The interviewing process includes seven steps:

1. *Prepare.* Thoroughly review the requirements and responsibilities of the job vacancy, as well as the necessary

qualifications of job applicants. Before each interview, study the applicant's resume, job application form, references or any other materials provided. Jot down any out-of-the-ordinary questions that come to mind and decide what approach you'll take in determining this person's job strengths and weaknesses. Finally, eliminate any distractions during the interview by shutting your office door and holding all telephone calls.

2. *Establish rapport.* Create an atmosphere that allows for free and relaxed discussion. Smile to make the job applicant feel welcome, use his or her first name and find some common topic of interest to get the interview off to a good start. Establishing rapport gives you the ability to more easily ask about sensitive areas of the applicant's background since he or she will be more likely to "open up" to you.

3. *Obtain information.* Ask questions of your applicant before giving information about job needs or requirements. Pose open-ended, probing questions about the applicant's work history, professional accomplishments and job strengths and weaknesses. Use caution, however, when asking about his or her personal life or family history.

4. *Maintain control.* This allows you to direct the flow of the conversation and dictate its length, while maintaining rapport with the interviewee. Don't hesitate to interrupt an applicant who rambles on and on. Similarly, don't feel obliged to answer questions asked by the applicant while you're still trying to obtain information.

5. *Give information.* Every job applicant is entitled to some information about your company, the responsibilities of the position, compensation, and working terms and conditions. However, by allowing the applicant to provide information first, you then can decide how much information to give based on your initial evaluation of the applicant.

6. *Close.* After providing the applicant with the information you deem necessary, end the interview by explaining what procedures remain

in the screening process and how long it will take you to fill the position. Always follow up each interview with a letter informing the applicant about your final hiring decision.

7. *Evaluate results.* This is usually the most difficult part of the employee selection process. To successfully evaluate potential employees you must examine characteristics like motivation, interest, achievement orientation, energy level and commitment. These characteristics may be just as important as the candidate's qualifications and existing knowledge of the job or industry.

Asking the Right Questions

During a job interview, it's vital to ask applicants the right questions to obtain all the information you need to make the right hiring decision. Failing to ask the right questions can cause job candidates to withhold pertinent information, which may work for or against them. While it may help candidates avoid sensitive areas of their job histories, it also may result in job strengths being overlooked.

There are five areas which should be explored with job applicants, especially those seeking managerial or professional positions.

1. *Technical competence:* Carefully probe the applicant's academic background. Pay particular attention to postgraduate education and training. Advanced degrees, adult education classes and professional training or certificates usually are good indicators of the quest for knowledge and the desire to succeed. Size up the responsibilities the candidate had on his or her last job. If applicable, ask to see samples of the candidate's work.

2. *Intellectual functioning:* This means more than looking at grades. What kind of college did the applicant attend? In addition to required courses, which electives did he or she take? The answers to these questions say a lot about the applicant's intellectual curiosity and pursuits. Carefully listen to the job candidate's responses to your questions. Just remember, although it's important

to hear what the person says, it's just as important to hear how he or she says it. In addition to verbal skills, check the job candidate's written communication.

3. *Energy and drive:* These attributes are particularly critical in a small business because there are fewer employees and each plays a bigger role in the success of the company. To gauge energy and drive, you must evaluate the job candidate's needs and motivations. They might be job security, the desire for achievement or simply self-fulfillment. People who are highly motivated set goals for themselves and have a strong need to achieve their objectives. Ask the job applicant about accomplishing these goals and objectives. Also discuss any challenges that have been taken on. Energetic people usually thrive on challenges.

4. *People skills:* These are not only important in dealing with team members and other co-workers, but also in establishing relationships with customers, suppliers and other business contacts. During the interview process, look for applicants who are sensitive, who understand people's motivations and needs and who engender respect from others both inside and outside the company. To analyze an applicant's people skills, ask about relationships with supervisors, peers and subordinates.

5. *Emotional maturity:* A job candidate who lacks emotional maturity in any way may suffer from the loss of objectivity, inconsistent behavior and lapses in judgement or good decision-making. During the interview, be wary of a job candidate's nervousness, lack of control or extreme intensity. Any evidence of extremes in behavior can indicate emotional immaturity or a character imbalance. Your goal should be to hire a well-balanced, well-rounded person who can handle difficult situations as they arise.

When someone gets high marks in all of these areas, it usually means the applicant is well qualified. However, depending upon the type of position being filled, high marks in one of the areas may be more critical.

The Importance of Background Checks

A thorough pre-employment background check will help insure that your top candidates for a job are truly qualified. These checks take time and effort and include several steps.

1. Ask each candidate to complete a job application form in his or her own handwriting and at your place of business. By doing this, you'll know if job applicants can read and write without assistance from others. If appropriate for the position being filled, ask each applicant to submit a resume.

2. Review the job candidate's work history, looking specifically for gaps in employment. These could signal a layoff, a dismissal, erratic work habits or even a criminal record. Ask the candidate to explain the circumstances surrounding any employment gaps.

3. Check for a prior criminal record, especially if the new hire will be handling money or a large inventory of products as part of his or her job duties. The law allows an employer to ask potential employees if they have been convicted of a felony, so this question should appear somewhere on your application form.

4. Conduct a credit check, if appropriate, to determine how the applicant has managed personal finances, including any late payments on credit cards or bills and any bankruptcy declarations. However, be careful when assessing this information and give the applicant a chance to explain the circumstances surrounding his or her financial difficulties. Because of the Fair Credit Reporting Act, an applicant usually must sign a release form in order for a hiring company to conduct the check. The company is then obligated to protect the confidentiality of the applicant's credit history.

5. Contact references listed on the job candidate's resume. Unfortunately, countless lawsuits filed by former employees have caused many businesses to eliminate their policy of providing references. Some will only confirm dates of employment and a former employee's title. To get

around this reluctance to provide more information, directly contact the applicant's former supervisor whenever possible or talk to former competitors who may be more willing to discuss the applicant's reputation.

6. Verify the candidate's educational experience by placing a quick telephone call to the registrar's office of the trade school, college or university that he or she attended. If the position being filled requires a professional license, confirm that the applicant actually has attained the necessary license. Whenever possible, also check with statewide professional groups to see if any complaints have been filed or actions have been taken against the job applicant.

7. Require the applicant to take pre-employment tests. For example, someone applying for a secretarial job usually is required to take a typing test, while someone applying for a job in a warehouse may be asked to prove that he or she can lift heavy objects. Because of employment discrimination laws such as the Americans with Disabilities Act, be sure that the tests given actually relate to the duties of the position.

8. Investigate if a job applicant has filed any Workers Compensation Claims, which can be enormously expensive for small business owners whose employees have been injured at work. However, not all states provide information about Workers Compensation claims for purposes of pre-employment screening.

9. Check the applicant's motor vehicle record if the position to be filled involves driving, especially the use of company cars or trucks.

Because of something called negligent hiring, it's more important than ever for companies to thoroughly investigate job applicants before they are hired. If a company fails to use good judgment when hiring or fails to check a new employee's background and that employee commits a crime or injures someone while on the job, the company can be held legally liable. The law of negligent hiring contends that the company should have known that its employee posed a threat. A very costly lawsuit often results.

In most cases, what's needed to complete a thorough background check on a job applicant is public information, with the exception of a credit report.

How to Get New Employees Off to a Fast Start

Sometimes busy supervisors and small business owners give little, if any, attention to orienting new employees. ***This is a serious mistake.*** Most people come to their new jobs with positive attitudes. They are generally excited about their new positions, yet often a bit nervous, too. A little extra time properly orienting new people can go a long way toward maximizing their long-term effectiveness on the job.

A Checklist for Orienting the New Worker

1. Welcome the employee.

2. Outline the philosophy and objectives of the organization.

3. Explain the organization's operations, the levels of authority and their relation.

4. Give a brief history of the organization.

5. Outline what is expected of the employee: attitude, reliability, initiative, emotional maturity, personal appearance.

6. Detail the employee's job functions and responsibilities.

7. Explain the pertinent rules, regulations, procedures and policies (also city, state and federal laws if applicable).

8. Introduce the employee to fellow workers.

9. Explain the criteria for performance appraisal.

10. Review promotional opportunities.

11. Outline the specific conditions of employment: working hours, punctuality, attendance, conduct, overtime, termination causes and procedures.

12. Explain pay periods, procedures and benefits: salary, insurance, sick time, rest breaks, vacation, recreation facilities, holidays, social activities, education benefits, pension, etc.

13. Explain use of safety devices, fire prevention, etc.

14. Reiterate your welcome and give encouragement.

Providing On-The-Job Training

Someone has just been hired or transferred at work and is to begin taking on some new responsibilities under your supervision. No matter how much education or experience the person has, he or she may not know how to do the work you must supervise. Your job, at that point, becomes providing on-the-job training (OJT). OJT is a difficult assignment since the person is new and feeling insecure. Your relationship with that individual hasn't really developed yet and since first impressions are important, this interaction could affect how things go between you in the weeks and months ahead. Here are some tips for showing someone how to do a new task.

Preparation of the Learner

Start with an orientation process. It should include these steps:

1. *Put the learner at ease.* Tell him or her how long it took you to learn the task and about the early errors you made. This reassures the person that your expectations are realistic, and it also relieves tension.

2. *Explain the "why" of the whole job.* Place it in the bigger picture and explain how it fits in with the other things going on at your workplace. Make the individual feel important and needed by others.

3. *Find out what the learner already knows about this kind of operation.* If he or she hasn't done anything exactly like it before, relate the tasks to something familiar by using an analogy. For example, "This computer is a lot like an ordinary typewriter," or, "It's like the remote control on your television."

4. *Provide the vocabulary you'll be using.* Identify the equipment, materials, tools and trade names involved.

Presentation of the Operation

Take the person through the steps of the operation in these stages:

1. Go through a sample operation at a normal pace. This shows the individual what it is you'll be teaching.

2. Go through the operation at a slow pace several times, explaining each step.

3. Between operations, explain the difficult parts or those in which errors are likely to be made. Explain quantity and quality requirements.

4. Go through the operation several times again at a slow pace. Illustrate the key points you just made.

5. Have the learner explain the steps to you as you again go through the operation at a slow pace.

6. Continue going through the operation until the learner demonstrates that she or he understands everything you are doing.

Performance Tryout

Let the learner do the job by following these steps:

1. Have the individual go through a sample task slowly, explaining aloud what he or she is doing at every step.

2. Go through a sample task again. This time correct whatever mistakes are being made and, if necessary, do some of the complicated steps that take longer to learn.

3. Next, you (the trainer) should run through a sample task at a normal pace.

4. Have the learner do the job, gradually building up skill and speed.

5. As soon as the learner demonstrates ability to do the job, let him or her do so but remain readily accessible for help.

Follow-Up

Complete the training process by following these steps:

1. Designate how the person can ask questions or receive help when necessary.

2. Gradually decrease supervision, checking the work from time to time against quantity and quality standards. Correct faulty work patterns before they become a habit.

3. Compliment, compliment, compliment the person after every successfully completed step!

A Formalized Mentor Program

At May Department Stores, topnotch college graduates are being recruited and integrated successfully into the company's executive ranks. One key element in this process is a mentor program. For the duration of the management trainee program (which can be one to two years long) each trainee is assigned to a senior executive. This way he or she not only learns the ins and outs of the business, but also sees firsthand the long-term potential of careers with May Department Stores.

The mentor program demonstrates the company's genuine interest in their recruits' futures with the firm. It also boosts morale among the executives who serve as mentors. The program relieves a problem that had accompanied the organization's intensified recruiting efforts: a strong sense of resentment among the older, more established executives toward the young, highly trained and ambitious recruits. After working directly with the trainees, the mentors' fears about the newest corporate comers were mitigated.

Job Design

Promotion by Poll

A supervisory position was open at a small steel plant. Two in-house candidates were available to fill it: One was the person with the most seniority, the other was a younger, less-experienced person of much greater ability. Management was unsure whom to choose.

The opening came up after a group of employees had complained so much about their foreman that he quit. Management wanted to promote the man with low seniority, but they feared that the older employees would resent such a move.

Eugene Benge, the plant's consultant, suggested using a survey to measure actual worker opinions. The 47 people to be affected by the decision were asked to designate on secret ballots their top three choices for foreman.

The young man that management favored received 38 first- place votes and was promoted.

By polling its employees, the company knew its decision was in harmony with worker opinion; it could use the poll results to support the decision to anyone who questioned it. Also, the new foreman felt wanted by his co-workers, and the workers felt that they had a voice in a decision of importance to them. So when you are in doubt about a choice that will strongly affect employee morale, consider using an anonymous survey to learn the true feelings of the employees.

Employees and Goals

George Odiorne, a leading consultant to many large organizations, recommends setting three kinds of goals. He suggests that managers and subordinates regularly discuss routine, problem-solving and innovative goals. Small business owners should do the same with their employees.

Routine goals refer to essential, recurring actions that can easily be counted and measured. Their effect is organizational stability. These goals generally appear in job descriptions.

Problem-solving goals refer to actions that will heal things that are not well, patch up holes, bind wounds and restore things to the status quo when they have gone astray from the normal routine. These are the goals that restore normality.

Innovative goals are the highest order of goals since they refer to actions that call for creation, invention and often high levels of technical competence — the kind that could change the character of the organization. They are essential to the growth of the firm.

According to Odiorne, these goals should help determine compensation. He believes:

1. If a subordinate is not attaining a minimum level of performance in his or her routine responsibilities, either the subordinate should not be retained in that position or he or she should be given training and time to improve.

2. If a subordinate is performing all routine duties but doing nothing more, he or she is fulfilling the job description and is entitled to the same job (at the same pay) for another year.

3. Raises and bonuses should go to the individual who is involved not only in fulfilling his or her routine duties but also in achieving problem-solving and innovative goals. He or she is worth more to the company.

Giving Constructive Criticism

As a supervisor or small business owner you face a very challenging situation when employees do something you don't like. You must decide whether the irritating behavior is more important than the risk and effort required to confront the person. Some people prefer to let things slide. For them, confrontation is very difficult. They know that people usually don't like being wrong and may object to their comments. But they also know that waiting to confront someone usually just escalates the problem. Knowing how to criticize someone effectively minimizes the negative repercussions of a confrontation. There are three key stages to giving constructive criticism:

PREPARATION • PRESENTATION • FOLLOW-UP

Preparation for Constructive Criticism

Reprimanding a person works best when you give it some forethought. The next time you must administer some criticism, take these steps:

- *Set an appropriate time and place.* Talk with the person as soon as possible after the event, but do so in private. Don't criticize someone in front of people — especially those people whose opinions that person values. The reaction you get will be for the onlookers' benefit and will distort your interaction.

- *Think through your opening comments in advance.* If possible, rehearse your initial statements aloud with someone you trust — perhaps a friend, your spouse or a fellow supervisor. If irritation has built up in your mind, you may find your initial comments loaded with anger. Venting some feelings first can defuse your hostility.

- *Think about the other person's view of the situation.* Ask your rehearsal partner to imagine both how the other person probably saw the incident and how that person might hear your criticism. Remember, people usually do what they think is best, so the behavior you are criticizing somehow made sense to that person at the time.

Presenting Your Criticism

When reprimanding someone:

- *Get to the point immediately.* Don't spend more than a minute or two in small talk — aimless chatter leaves the other person guessing and he or she will probably misinterpret the purpose of the meeting. Instead, first identify the incident you are addressing, next describe how you saw it, then explain why you think the individual's behavior was not what it should have been.

- *Ask whether the other person understands the points you've made so far.* Then, get his or her perspective. Ask for the reasoning behind the actions. (Be prepared to learn from that — you may have misinterpreted something.)

- *Focus on the future*. What's happened is "water under the bridge." Concentrate on what can be learned from this incident. Emphasize that your concern is not to scold or punish, but to make the organization work more effectively in the future. Be specific about what behavior you would prefer from that individual the next time a similar situation arises and explain why you believe that that alternative would yield a better outcome. Check whether the other person understands and agrees to do what you are proposing. Genuine agreement is better than forced compliance.

Following Up on Criticism

No matter how considerate you attempt to be, a confrontation is still experienced as a putdown unless you follow it up properly.

- *Be positive about the individual* even though you are being negative about that person's specific behavior. Mention the things he or she does that you value and appreciate. Position yourself on the person's side — say that above all you want things to work out well for the individual in your organization and you know they can.

- *Emphasize that, for you, the past is past and you are expecting good things to occur in the future.* If appropriate, set a meeting for a time after a few actions of the kind you criticized are likely to happen again. When you meet, you can assess how things are going. This follow-up meeting will give you a chance to check on progress, nip any new problems in the bud and catch the person doing things right!

Performance Appraisals

William Scherkenbach, Ford Motor Company's Director of Statistical Methods, points out a serious drawback in most performance appraisal systems. He maintains that they reduce initiative and risk-taking. They encourage what he calls the Alexiev Mentality.

You may recall that Vassily Alexiev was a Russian super-heavyweight weightlifter. He was paid a sum of money for each world record he broke. Being a disciplined athlete, he broke a lot of world records. But, being a smart person too, he broke them only a few grams at a time.

The Alexiev Mentality is encouraged by performance appraisal systems that are based on whether or not employees achieve their objectives. Because of the penalty for failing to make objectives and because objectives typically are negotiated, employees end up with goals that don't have much "stretch" or are relatively easy to achieve.

Another factor contributing to the Alexiev Mentality is fear of the unknown. A person may know of ways to achieve an eight percent savings in one year. However, he or she is required by the agreed-upon objectives to attain only a five percent savings each year. What happens by the end of the year? He or she shows a five percent savings. He or she banks the additional three percent for the next year so that the objective for that year can be met.

What's the alternative? Scherkenbach believes it is appraising people on broader criteria than specific individual objectives. He recommends evaluating employees on all of their contributions "to the continuous improvement of the company."

How to Conduct Performance Appraisals

On the surface it would seem that evaluating employee performance ought to be fairly easy. After all, performance appraisals should be tied directly to job success. The hang-up comes in creating realistic and appropriate measures for determining job success.

There are a number of pitfalls you'll want to avoid as you evaluate employee performance.

- *Avoid the "halo" effect where a high rating on a favored trait adds unmerited points in other areas.*

- *Be sure to rate the worker only for performance on the current job.* Don't let work on a previous job color your evaluation either positively or negatively.

- *Rate the employee through the entire period covered by the evaluation.* Don't let the performance of the last two weeks unduly influence you. Don't let a months-old incident weigh too heavily, either.

- *Avoid the tendency to give an "average" rating on each point.* Part of the objective for performance appraisals is to point out "soft spots" for further development. Across-the board average marks hide these.

- *Try to hold separate sessions for performance appraisal and salary review.* The appraisal interview should focus on performance considerations only.

Questions the Supervisor or Small Business Owner Should Answer Before the Performance Appraisal

1. What specific points can you praise the employee for?

2. What are the specific areas in which you want the employee to improve?

3. Can you support your evaluation of the employee's performance with hard facts?

4. What specific improvement(s) do you want to see?

5. What kind of help or training can you offer?

6. What kind of follow-up do you have planned?

The Goals of the Performance Appraisal

1. To provide the worker with a precise understanding of how you feel the worker is performing

2. To provide the worker with a clear understanding about what performance is expected on the job

3. To establish a mutually agreed-upon program of performance improvement

4. To develop a stronger working relationship between the supervisor or small business owner and the worker.

Try Appraising Yourself

An organization can only be as effective as the flow of messages it permits. Higher-level managers and some small business owners have an especially difficult time learning what their subordinates honestly think. Employees often fear saying anything negative to higher-ups — they assume bosses aren't interested, already have the information or they fear being penalized for "negative" thinking or "whistleblowing."

Reginald Jones, an outstanding CEO at General Electric, used an effective method for getting feedback from subordinates on his own performance.

The corporation's top officers held an annual meeting to review business conditions and the performance of its managers. On the final day, an informal dinner was held.

Jones retired to his room and did not attend the dinner. But he designated as its host a well-respected, long-term officer of the company — a sort of elder statesperson whose integrity was unquestioned.

The ground rules for the dinner were that the participants would engage in a frank, no-holds-barred discussion of the corporation's performance under Jones and of Jones' leadership.

Everything was to be off the record, and then no one was ever to mention the dinner to Jones except the elder statesperson.

The morning after the dinner, Jones met for several hours with the host to go over the previous evening's discussion. No names were mentioned, but the full critique of Jones' leadership strengths and weaknesses was presented to him.

Jones had to be a strong person to subject himself to this probing review. But his willingness may be an indication of why he was selected by his peers as America's most admired chief executive.

Consider identifying someone in your organization who can solicit for you candid feedback from subordinates about your performance. Be sure that person maintains confidentiality.

4

HANDLING EMPLOYMENT ISSUES

Even though you've learned how to become an effective leader, build a working team and get the most out of your team members, you'll still encounter some roadblocks along the path to success. It's an inevitable part of being a supervisor or a small business owner. This chapter will show you how to handle some of those bumps and curves in the road.

Handling Complaints

Supervisors and small business owners frequently have to serve as "flak-catchers." They are held accountable for whatever they do and for whatever their team members do. When people feel dissatisfied about a unit's services or products, they usually contact the person in charge to complain. Talking face-to-face with someone who has a gripe about your area of responsibility or your company usually is very unpleasant. Many supervisors and small business owners either avoid it (usually by having their secretary screen such calls) or get annoyed at complainers and react defensively. Flak-catching can be handled effectively, however, if you react appropriately.

The key skill here is not letting a complaint make you feel personally attacked, scolded or insulted. To avoid this reaction, listen to complaints as messages about how people perceived the situation. Here are some suggestions:

1. *Complainers should be perceived as doing you a favor.* For every person who takes the trouble to voice a complaint, many others who are dissatisfied simply take their business elsewhere. And those unhappy people usually tell many others what happened and warn them against dealing with you. So complainers are giving you a second chance which the others didn't even offer. They also provide information you need to avoid making similar errors in the future. Hence, complaints actually need to be appreciated and heard as suggestions for improvement.

2. *Complaints may inform you about expectations of which you were unaware.* Complaints are about violated expectations. People maintain order in their lives by expecting certain things to occur in a predictable way. When people complain, they usually are telling you that they expected one thing and something else occurred instead. Sometimes those expectations match yours, and you see clearly the validity of the complaint. Sometimes, however, they are based on misunderstandings — you never intended to do what they expected — you didn't have the same view of the situation. So when someone complains, ask: "What did you expect?" and, "What led you to expect that?" You are likely to get information that leads to the root of the problem.

3. *Remember that violated expectations evoke stress that must be released.* Related stressful events have a cumulative effect. When a string of disappointments occurs, the next person around may get the brunt of them all. An emotional complaint you receive may be the result of a series of similar, frustrating incidents for which you were not responsible. When you are hit with a surprisingly vehement

complaint, consider what other stresses are packaged up with that one and being vented. Beware of perceiving complaints about a bundle of life's mishaps as an attack on you. To learn what triggered the person's temper, ask, "What other incidents does this problem remind you of?" Let the other party blow off steam. Then, separate what you did from the actions for which you are not responsible.

4. *Complainers tend to assume that whatever happened was done intentionally.* For example, when someone is slow to respond to a letter or phone call, people conjure up an explanation for that delay. That explanation usually assumes intentionality — that you are deliberately avoiding contact — although the letter or phone message may never have reached you. Therefore, beware that errors you see as being due to circumstances beyond your control will be viewed by others as "your fault." They will believe that you could have prevented the error if you really wanted to, so they will address you as the kind of person who would deliberately allow such a thing to occur. The complaint that emerges, naturally, will sound like a personal accusation or insult. Don't respond by counterattacking. Just explain your perspective and emphasize that if, indeed, you had been able to control things, they wouldn't have turned out as they did.

The Supervisor and the Labor Contract

Supervisors in a unionized organization have a dual responsibility, as do small business owners with union employees. First, as a member of management, they must work toward achieving the maximum productivity from workers. Second, the supervisor must be aware of and adhere to management's commitments under the union contract. The organization will be held accountable for the supervisor's failure to uphold the agreements between management and the union. The small business owner faces the same responsibilities.

The Labor-Management Relations Act of 1947 outlines unfair labor practices affecting the supervisor or small business owner. Predominant among these are:

1. Blocking employee efforts to form or join a union

2. Attempting to influence a labor union

3. Discriminating against the members of a union

4. Discriminating against a worker for bringing a charge against an employer under this Labor-Management Relations Act

The Grievance Process

Many times it is to the advantage of all concerned if a grievance is settled at the supervisory level. It promotes management confidence in the supervisor, develops an atmosphere of cooperation without costly arbitration between the union and management and prevents minor problems from becoming major problems that hurt morale and cause disruption.

Yet, not every grievance should be settled this way. Unusual situations or grievances that affect a large number of employees should go to a higher management level or to the personnel department. In any case, the supervisor should never try to block any part of the grievance process.

The Steps in a Typical Grievance Procedure

1. The worker, the union steward and the supervisor discuss the grievance.

2. The grievance is discussed by the supervisor's superior and the union grievance committee.

3. The union grievance committee, the manager of the local organization and its industry relations manager evaluate the grievance.

4. The grievance is discussed by the union grievance committee, the organization's top general management, industrial relations manager and national union representatives.

5. The grievance is discussed by top management and national union representatives.

6. The grievance is referred to a mutually agreed-upon arbitrator for final resolution.

How to Avoid Most Grievance Problems

1. Develop an understanding of labor law, the union contract, past accepted practice and your responsibilities as a supervisor or small business owner.

2. Promote a good working relationship with the union steward.

3. Create as fair a work environment as possible.

4. Keep an open mind and encourage discussion of problems.

5. Investigate the cause of each complaint.

6. Evaluate the facts surrounding the issue.

7. Determine a course of action to remedy the problem.

8. Advise all personnel who will be affected by your solution *before* it is implemented.

9. Follow up on the results and side effects of the solution.

Supervising Minority Workers

First of all, what is a minority worker? The common usage of the term *minority worker* refers to an employee who is a member of a certain racial, age or disabled group. Also, female employees (even though they constitute almost 50 percent of the work force) are usually considered minority workers.

Pertinent Laws Affecting Minority Employees

• *Title VII of the Civil Rights Act of 1964, as amended by the Equal Employment Opportunity Act of 1972*, prohibits discrimination based on race, color, religion, sex or national origin in any term, condition or privilege of employment. This law applies to all private employers of 15 or more people, all public and private educational institutions, all state and local governments, all public and private employment agencies, labor unions with 15 or more members and joint labor-management committees for apprenticeships and training.

• *Title VI of the 1964 Civil Rights Act* prohibits discrimination based on race, color or national origin in all programs of activities that receive federal financial aid in order to provide employment.

• *The Equal Pay Act passed in 1963 and later amended by Title IX of the Educational Amendments Act of 1972* requires all employers covered by the Fair Labor Standards Act (and others included in the 1972 extension) to provide equal pay to men and women who perform work that is similar in skill, effort and responsibility. Title VII of the Act (and others included in the 1972 extension) provide equal pay to men and women who perform work that is similar in skill, effort and responsibility. Title VII of the Civil Rights Act also requires equal pay regardless of race, national origin or sex. This includes base pay as well as opportunities for overtime, raises, bonuses, commissions and other benefits. Offering and paying higher wages to women and minorities in order to attract these groups is also illegal.

• *The Rehabilitation Act of 1973* prohibits employers from denying jobs to individuals merely because of a handicap. This law applies to government contractors and subcontractors with contracts of $50,000 or more and 50 or more employees.

• *Title IX of the Education Amendments Act of 1972* prohibits discrimination against people between the ages of 40 and 70 in any area of employment and applies to employers of 25 or more people.

• *Executive Order 11246, amended by Executive Order 11375 in 1967*, requires federal contractors and subcontractors to have affirmative action programs to increase employment opportunities for women and minorities in all areas of employment.

• **The Civil Rights Act of 1991** overturns several recent Supreme Court decisions and gives the following important rights to discrimination claimants:

1. The act expands the Civil Rights Act of 1866 and specifically covers all forms of race discrimination, including racial harassment on the job and other post-employment actions, as well as hiring decisions.

2. The act expands civil rights remedies in cases of intentional discrimination, and claimants can now recover compensatory and punitive damages, as well as back pay, in religious, sex or disability discrimination under the act. Previously, only claims of racial or ethnic bias provided such relief.

3. When a claimant seeks compensatory or punitive damages under Title VII, either the plaintiff or the employer can demand a jury trial.

4. New demands are placed on the employer when a "protected group" employee is disproportionately affected by an employment practice. The employer must now show that the challenged practice is "job-related to the position and consistent with business necessity."

5. The act prohibits mixed motive discrimination by making it unlawful for an employer to rely on a discriminatory factor in an employment-related decision, even if other nondiscriminatory factors also justified the employer's decision.

6. The act expands the time limit in which an employee may file a seniority system claim to 300 days.

7. The act allows an employer to "give and act upon the results of any professionally developed ability test provided that such test, its administration or action upon the results, is not designed, intended or used to discriminate because of race, color, religion, sex or national origin." The act makes it unlawful for employers to adjust scores, use different cut-off scores for or otherwise alter the results of employment-related tests on the basis of members of protected groups.

- **The Family and Medical Leave Act of 1993** requires private employers with 50 or more employees to provide eligible employees with up to 12 weeks of unpaid leave for their own serious illnesses, for the birth or adoption of a child or the care of a seriously ill child, spouse or parent. The new law is scheduled to take effect on August 5, 1994. For companies with collective bargaining agreements, the law becomes effective on the date the contract expires or one year after the date the law was enacted — February 5, 1994 — whichever comes first.

In addition to these federal laws affecting employment, many cities and states have passed legislation regarding another minority concern — sexual orientation.

How to Create a Positive Equal Employment Opportunity Atmosphere

1. Be aware of the legal and regulatory requirements of Equal Employment Opportunity (EEO) and affirmative action that affect your organization.

2. Be aware of your organization's policies and practices that have resulted from EEO and affirmative action regulation.

3. Learn to recognize and eliminate stereotyping and preconceptions in your expectations of women and minorities.

4. Provide clear, challenging and achievable expectations for all of your subordinates.

5. Provide training, support and encouragement that fit individual needs.

6. Be aware of and sensitive to issues that commonly arise in work forces comprised of different groups.

7. Help to facilitate the socialization of new employees.

8. Communicate with your employees to minimize isolation and maximize the contribution of all employees.

9. Provide adequate feedback on performance for all employees.

10. Avoid the extremes of "overprotection" and "abandonment" in dealing with minority group members.

Managing Stress

Someone at work seems edgy, hypersensitive to criticism, is easily discouraged or has poor concentration and a short attention span. You may see that individual eating, smoking or drinking too much. Be slow to condemn that person — he or she probably is overstressed. In fact . . . that individual might be you! Whether stress is someone else's problem or yours, you need to know how to deal with it. Otherwise, living under stress leads to poor health, being accident-prone, making errors and impulsive, poor decisions.

The key factor affecting stress in the workplace is having control over one's circumstances. Here's why.

Some stress is natural. People thrive on dealing with challenging situations. But they also need relief periodically. When they can't control the presence of stressful conditions, when relief isn't available when needed, they begin to lose their ability to cope and become exhausted. That condition is commonly called "burnout."

But having too little stress is also harmful. Repetitious, unchallenging work leads to the opposite effect, being bored too much of the time or "rustout."

To function at one's best is to operate at a level of optimal stress. That state of high motivation, energy and enthusiasm has been called working at your own ideal "flow."

How do supervisors and small business owners help their people and themselves avoid burnout and rustout — to work at their optimal or "flow" levels?

There are two major approaches:

1. Changing *external* conditions

2. Changing *internal* conditions

Changing External Conditions

When people can speed up or slow down the pace of external input, they can manage stress effectively. The following working conditions might need to become more flexible or supportive for someone feeling overstressed:

- *Break Time* — People feeling too much unrelenting pressure may need to be given more leeway to relax, stretch and shift gears when they feel the need.

- *Bureaucracy* — People who feel that they are overwhelmed with tedious procedures that interfere with getting important things done may need to have some "red tape" cut.

- *Time Off* — People who are experiencing particularly hard times in their personal lives (such as a divorce or death in the family) may need to be given a lighter load for awhile until they have adjusted to the stressful changes such events bring.

- *Social Support* — People having a hard time meeting the current demands of their work or their personal lives may need someone to listen and understand and help them think of alternate ways to handle what they are going through.

- *Freedom from Delays and Rushing* — People whose work is subject to excessive delays or rush orders may need help restructuring their schedule to minimize these stress-producing time pressures.

Changing Internal Conditions

When work conditions frequently evoke stress and can't be changed, people can use these methods to influence their own inner state so they do not become overwhelmed.

- *Relaxation* — Muscular tension accompanies stress, so breaking for a couple of minutes to take some deep breaths and to stretch out one's muscles helps unwind a tight body.

- *Physical Activity* — Being sedentary allows stress to build up in the body. Walking around periodically or doing some physical exercise during a work break or over the lunch hour helps relieve stress.

- *Mental Imagery* — When worrisome work responsibilities fill one's mind, stress builds up. Picturing the successful outcome of a project or picturing pleasant images, such as one's family or an upcoming vacation, replaces stress-producing images with positive, energizing thoughts.

- *Being Assertive* — When you are victimized by a work situation that overloads you with stress, you can help yourself by taking the initiative to call your predicament to your supervisor's or small business owner's attention and proposing reasonable ways that your work conditions can be improved.

A Stop Button

The Japanese have, in their auto assembly plants, a "stop button." It's a quality control measure. Assembly line workers can stop the whole line any time they find a defect in what they are producing.

This is only one part of a general "self-inspection" policy. All workers are expected to monitor quality, and they are given the power to do something about it independently when they spot a potential problem.

You might tell your employees that they each have the power to push a "stop button" any time they notice something going wrong. Establish a clear and safe way they can halt any operation when they notice something not being done properly.

What to Do When Personal Problems Affect Job Performance

Red Flags to Watch for

Be alert to and document the *problem* and/or *changes* in employee behavior in these areas:

1. Unexcused absences

2. Unexcused tardiness

3. Violations of the law

4. Possessing or using drugs on company premises

5. Leaving work without permission

6. Safety violations

7. Dress code violations

8. Garnishment of wages

9. Insubordination

10. Fighting

11. Reduced productivity

12. Increased error rate

How to Confront the Employee

1. *Confront the employee with a specific critique of his or her performance.* Now is the time to bring out your documented evidence of unsatisfactory performance. Remember, restrict your comments and discussion to the issues surrounding the employee's job performance. Your job is not to sermonize on the negative effects of drug abuse or other problems. If the employee wants to talk about his or her personal problems, listen. Your advice to the employee should be limited to how to get help.

2. *Refer the employee to counseling and assistance.* Be prepared for angry or defensive behavior by the employee. Emphasize that admitting the problem and accepting help will not jeopardize the employee's job. Also assure the employee that your discussion and all aspects of the assistance program are confidential. Be able to provide information about insurance coverage or other financial assistance that is available. Many large companies have employee assistance programs in place to help workers deal with difficult issues.

3. *Address the need for performance improvement.* If appropriate to your situation and if the employee accepts help, you might agree to a schedule of performance improvements. If help is refused, inform the employee of the consequences. Very often, if help is refused and performance is not improved, termination would be the consequence. The worker should also understand that performance improvement must be maintained in order to avoid disciplinary action or termination.

Monitoring Progress of Recovering Employees

1. *Continue to document the employee's job performance.* Note both problems and improvements.

2. *Emphasize that continued and serious participation in the employee assistance program is necessary to avoid discipline or termination.*

3. *Be aware of and follow the employee assistance program guidelines for rehabilitation expectations.*

4. *Do not ignore performance/behavior problems because the employee is recovering.* Corrective action should be taken when the employee doesn't perform adequately.

5. *Be watchful for and encourage improvement on the part of the employee.*

6. *Continue to protect the confidentiality of the employee's personal problems and the assistance program.* While it is

your responsibility to inform upper management of the employee's participation in an assistance program, sharing information of a specific nature concerning the employee's problems with anyone is unethical and would leave you open to legal action.

7. *Never give out nonprescription drugs (cough syrup, aspirin, etc.) to recovering employees.* It's not a good idea to dispense medication of any kind to any employee because of the potential negative side effects for which you and/or the organization might be held liable.

Handling Absenteeism and Tardiness

First, the facts. Did you know...

• Workers with high rates of absenteeism and tardiness during their first years of employment usually maintain higher-than average rates through succeeding years?

• Even though health levels in general are higher, job absenteeism has increased in the last few years?

• Absenteeism generally is higher on Mondays, Fridays and before or after holidays?

• The percentage of absenteeism in large companies is greater than small companies?

• Commuting distance doesn't appear to be related to absenteeism?

• The rate of absenteeism in factories is roughly twice that in offices?

What You Can Do to Limit Absenteeism

1. *First of all, have an attendance policy.* Point out that regular attendance is required. Stipulate that advance notice of absence be given when possible. Make sure employees know whom to notify of an absence. (Generally, it is their immediate supervisor.)

2. *Let employees know of their importance in accomplishing company and departmental goals.* Emphasize how the work of the organization suffers when they are absent.

3. *Address the issue.* Require all employees who are absent to report to you before starting work. This gives you a chance to discover the real reasons for the absence and counsel the employee.

4. *Keep records.* Maintain an individual record for each worker that shows all absences, their length, the date of notification and reason.

5. *Allow time for personal business.* Employees sometimes feel compelled to call in sick in order to conduct a matter of personal business. Under the condition that advance notice be given, it is a good idea to allow your workers a certain amount of time off to handle personal matters.

Tardiness

The causes and cures for tardiness are similar to those of absenteeism. The previous five steps can be adapted to address tardiness issues with your workers.

Even more than absenteeism, tardiness — if not handled early on — can become a habit. It is important to confront the employee immediately, determine whether the tardiness is avoidable or unavoidable and note the cause. Chronic latecomers should be made aware of the seriousness of the situation and agree with you on a plan to remedy the problem. If the tardiness continues, be prepared to take disciplinary action.

How to Shape Up Problem Workers

Redirecting Problem Workers with Positive Discipline

The discipline you apply should be aimed at correcting behavior or performance, not punishing the employee. If the correction can be accomplished by a friendly discussion with the employee, so much the better. Likewise, oral or written warnings are less costly and problematic than a suspension from work. The disciplinary step of last resort — termination — is the most costly and least positive alternative of all.

Sequence of Disciplinary Steps

1. Oral warning not recorded in employee's personnel records
2. Oral warning recorded in employee's personnel records
3. Written reprimand
4. Suspension without pay
5. Termination

The "Hot Stove" Rule for Applying Discipline

Applying positive, corrective discipline is often compared to the burn received when touching a hot stove. The similarities are immediacy, advance warning, consistency and impartiality.

1. *A hot stove burns immediately.* Similarly, discipline should be applied quickly after an infraction. There should be no question in an employee's mind as to cause and effect.

2. *A hot stove radiates heat and gives a preliminary warning.* So should discipline.

3. *A hot stove always burns when touched.* Discipline also must be applied consistently.

4. *A hot stove plays no favorites.* Neither should discipline.

Pre-Discipline Checklist

1. Be aware of the law, the union contract (if any) and the policies and accepted practice of the organization.

2. Keep good records.

3. Investigate rule violations and the circumstances surrounding the incident.

4. Keep the union informed (if applicable).

5. Apply discipline as soon as possible.

6. Precede formal discipline with a warning.

7. Be consistent to all.

8. Relate the discipline to the violation, not the person.

9. Discipline in private.

10. Warn of the consequences of repeat offenses.

Typical Causes for Disciplinary Action

Absenteeism	Horseplay
Tardiness	Fighting
Leaving work station	Refusal of job assignment
Insubordination	Gambling
Mishandling of customers	Negligence
Using or possessing drugs	Dishonesty
or intoxicants	Theft
Damage to or loss of	Disloyalty
company property	Refusal to work overtime
Incompetence	Loafing
Low productivity	

When Employees Must Be Dismissed

For supervisors and small business owners probably the hardest part of their jobs involves firing an employee. While most companies have dismissal procedures that must be followed, small business owners must develop their own plans.

Employee Dismissal Checklist

When faced with the reality of firing an employee, you should follow these basic guidelines.

1. *Conduct the termination interview in private, never in public.*

2. *Make sure you aren't terminating the person on a holiday, birthday, anniversary or other important date.* The only exceptions are cases when company safety is at stake.

3. *Avoid dismissing an employee on Friday afternoon.* Give the person an opportunity to start looking for a new job right away.

4. *Insure that you have evaluated, counseled and warned the employee several times that a dismissal was possible.* Each instance should have been recorded and fully documented. Ask the employee to initial each instance of warning to make sure that he or she heard and understood the message.

5. *Insure that job performance expectations and compliance with company regulations were clarified when the employee was hired.*

6. *Plan carefully what you will say during the termination interview.* Include an opening, middle and close.

7. *Remain calm during the termination interview regardless of what the employee does.*

8. *Identify honestly the specific actions and behaviors that led to the termination.*

9. *Encourage the employee to talk to you and make sure he or she understands why the termination is warranted.*

10. *Determine if the terminated employee poses any threat to you or your organization.* If you don't trust the employee to leave peacefully, request security support. If you suspect that the employee may try to take company documents, equipment or other materials, escort him or her to his office and personally supervise the packing of personal belongings.

11. *Ask the employee to surrender his or her company identification badge, parking pass, keys or any other items that might allow access to the company.*

12. *Don't terminate an employee by telephone, letter or a pink slip placed in a paycheck.*

13. *Treat the terminated employee with dignity.*

14. *Keep the termination interview as short as possible.* Don't prolong the pain of the situation for either of you.

Providing Economic Support

Although many companies offer severance pay to terminated employees, the amount of pay may vary according to the nature of the dismissal and his or her years of service. Therefore, an employee who has worked for a company for 25 years likely will receive more pay than one who has been employed only two or three years. A common formula used to determine the amount of severance pay is one week's pay for each year of service.

In addition to severance pay, some companies will continue to provide terminated employees with medical benefits for a specified period of time, usually no longer than six months.

Using Outplacement Services

While it's an unpleasant task for the supervisor or small business owner handling the dismissal, it's potentially devastating to the person losing his or her job. Someone who has been fired usually goes through a wide range of emotions — first feeling hurt, then confused and finally resentful.

When resentment sets in, the dismissed employee may consider a lawsuit, invoking one of the Equal Employment Opportunity regulations that prohibits a firing because of age, sex, race or other factors. Another possibility is that the dismissed employee may speak out against his or her former company, its management and products and services. These comments really can hurt a company's established reputation within the business community. The dismissed employee also could have proprietary knowledge about the company's products or services which could be valuable to competitors.

For all of these reasons and because of an obligation to fairly treat a dismissed employee, supervisors and small business owners should make the parting as easy and amicable as possible. Career continuation or outplacement service is one way to accomplish that. In fact, outplacement has become as common as severance pay in today's termination packages for those employees in the mid- to upper-level managerial and professional ranks.

Generally outplacement is not offered to blue-collar or hourly employees. However, many unions have bargained for and won educational or re-training assistance for members who have lost their jobs due to termination or layoffs.

For those who are eligible, outplacement services are provided by many different firms in many different ways. Outplacement consultants operate much like attorneys or accountants. They are paid for the time they invest on various projects. Fees for full-time outplacement service at a reputable firm may represent from 10 to 15 percent of the terminated employee's compensation level. For a mid-level manager in the $30,000 to $50,000 salary range, the fee may be $3,000 to $5,000, plus expenses.

While some large national outplacement firms may have set programs for outplacement, many smaller outplacement firms offer customized or modified programs that can be tailored to a business' specific needs and available budget.

For instance, a dismissed employee may need help with a resume and development of a mailing campaign, as well as counseling on how to target companies for employment opportunities, how to interview effectively and how to network. On the other hand, he or she may not need an office and clerical support automatically provided by many large outplacement firms.

If your small business is in the market for an outplacement firm, the best advice is to shop around. Make sure that you talk to at least two or three reputable outplacement firms and that you evaluate the consultant or consultants who will be assigned to your project. If affordability is an issue, structure your own program rather than rely on a full-service outplacement program.

TIME MANAGEMENT

United Airlines makes a clever handout available to its staff called "A Round Tuit." It is a single sheet of paper which has a large circle on it. Inside the circle is the following message:

"This is a Round Tuit. Guard it with your life! Tuits are hard to come by — especially the round ones. It will help you to become a much more efficient worker. For years you have heard people say, 'I'll do this when I get a Round Tuit.' So, now that you have one, you can accomplish all those things you have put aside because now you have a Round Tuit."

Create your own Round Tuit and give it to someone who has put off doing something important. It will convey your message in a humorous way.

How Time Is Spent

In 1973, author Henry Mintzberg published a book *The Nature of Managerial Work*, which determined that a manager's daily activities are characterized by "brevity, variety and fragmentation." Although Mintzberg studied the comings and goings of five successful CEOs of large companies, his findings probably don't vary much from the daily schedules of most supervisors and small business owners.

Mintzberg found that 49 percent of these CEOs' daily encounters lasted less than nine minutes, while only 10 percent lasted more than an hour. When they weren't in scheduled meetings, the CEOs spent their time talking on the phone (average time: six minutes per call), walking through the office (average time: 11 minutes per walk), participating in unscheduled meetings (average time: 12 minutes per meeting) and working on routine office tasks (average time: 15 minutes per task). Overall, 78 percent of the CEOs' time was spent talking with people.

What this study shows and what other management experts say is that supervisors, and similarly small business owners, should spend most of their work days interacting with their team members. People skills should be most important to people in these positions.

How to Be an Effective Delegator

Many supervisors are promoted into their positions from "the trenches." Often they are more used to (and more comfortable with) performing the technical functions required to get the work done. As supervisors, though, their success is dependent on the work of others—the people they supervise. Small business owners must operate in much the same way.

Successful delegation includes three basic steps:

1. *Assigning* the work to the appropriate team member

2. *Gaining* the agreement and commitment of the worker to perform the duties satisfactorily for the supervisor

3. *Granting* the appropriate authority to the worker to take the actions necessary to complete the task

Overcoming the Most Common Obstacles to Delegation

1. *Fear of making a subordinate look too good.* The measure of a supervisor is almost entirely based upon the performance of those supervised. It's not what you do that counts, it is what you get done. The only way to get the most done is by making sure that your employees are encouraged, challenged and equipped with everything they need to be as effective and productive as they can be.

2. *"I'd better do it myself."* Many managers and supervisors short-circuit their supervisory potential by taking on work that should be done by their employees. Their excuse is, "If I want it done right, I'd better do it myself." It may be true. There may be many jobs that you actually can do better than anyone you could delegate to, but that is not the point. You can't be effective as a supervisor or small business owner and do your employees' work, too. And, beyond that, you can't expect your people to get as good at a task as you until they've had the chance to learn by making their own mistakes — probably the same way you learned.

3. *Wanting to look busy.* Some supervisors hoard work that should have been delegated in order to be (or appear to be) constantly busy. Their desire is to set a good example for the workers. A better example would be set by a supervisor who shows good self-management skills by working on what's really the most important and appropriate task at hand.

4. *Working on what "feels good."* Supervisors often are promoted into their positions because of their effectiveness at various jobs in their departments or companies. New supervisors, in particular, may find themselves chained to the old tasks that they can perform with more confidence and comfort.

5. *Preconceived ideas about employee abilities.* Supervisors and small business owners should avoid preconceptions about the abilities (or lack of abilities) of their employees. Even a worker who has not been successful in the past may perform very well with a new task under new circumstances.

Many supervisors and small business owners feel they do not have enough time in their workday to do all they have to do. However, the problem usually isn't the amount of time available, but the use to which that available time is being put. A number of time management problems are common . . . and fortunately, solutions exist for minimizing them.

Time-Wasters

Here are some items that cause supervisors and small business owners to lose precious workday time. Check those that apply to you.

_____ 1. Telephone interruptions that disrupt work progress

_____ 2. Visitors who drop by unexpectedly

_____ 3. Meetings that accomplish little

_____ 4. Crisis situations for which no contingency planning has been done

_____ 5. Putting effort into small things while high priority matters go unattended

_____ 6. Personal disorganization requiring time to find things when they are needed

_____ 7. Doing routine tasks that others could do equally well

_____ 8. Trying to do too much at once and underestimating the time things will take

_____ 9. Work "falling between the cracks" or being duplicated unnecessarily due to confusion about lines of authority and responsibility

_____ 10. An inability to say "no" to others

Research indicates that most people fall prey to at least half of these things. Thankfully, the effect of each can be reduced with specific time management techniques.

Time-Savers

Here are some ways that efficient supervisors and small business owners operate. Check the steps you could take to manage time more effectively.

_____ 1. Having a secretary or receptionist screen incoming calls and take messages on calls you need not take right away

_____ 2. Setting aside a specific time every day for returning calls

_____ 3. Getting right to the point on the phone or with visitors

_____ 4. Setting a specific time aside each day for drop-in visitors or unexpected events

_____ 5. Encouraging people to make appointments when they want to see you rather than simply stopping by unannounced

_____ 6. Personally making decisions, when appropriate, rather than referring them to a committee

_____ 7. When calling a meeting — setting an agenda and distributing it in advance

_____ 8. Drawing up a daily list of things to do and arranging them in priority order so you give the greatest amount of time to truly important areas

_____ 9. Determining the times of day when you work best and then taking on your most important projects during those times

_____ 10. Setting aside quiet time for yourself every day to reflect on what has happened over the past couple of days and plan the upcoming day

_____ 11. Delegating work and avoiding the tendency to do, your self, what others should be doing

_____ 12. Doing less pleasant tasks first, before the tasks you enjoy doing. This way, the enjoyable tasks serve as an incentive for getting the unpleasant tasks done

_____ 13. Trying to avoid handling any piece of paper more than once by acting on things as they come up

____   14.   Making efficient use of tidbits of time (such as time spent waiting in other people's offices) by doing small things such as responding to letters or reading magazine articles you've clipped out beforehand

Time Management Tools

To make the most of your time at work, you need to get organized. Here are some simple tools and tips to help you do just that.

- **Your desk** — Use it for writing, reading, sorting, storing work materials, filing frequently used materials and placement of your in-basket and out-basket. Do not use it for stacking papers, reading materials "you'll get around to," old reports or unopened mail.

    Tip 1:   Remove as many items as possible from your desk at the end of the day.
    Tip 2:   Use an in-basket and an out-basket to keep current work separated from completed work and tasks not yet begun.
    Tip 3:   Store office supplies such as paper, pens, pencils, scissors, stapler and tape in a drawer.
    Tip 4:   Situate your desk in a place where it's most pleasant and comfortable to work.

- **Your calendar** — Because there are several different styles, select one that best suits your needs. You may need two calendars: one for the office and one that you carry in a briefcase or purse.

    Tip 1:   Update all your calendars on a daily basis.
    Tip 2:   Include relevant information when adding an appointment or event to your calendar.
    Tip 3:   Establish some guidelines for scheduling if you have a secretary or an assistant.
    Tip 4:   Review your calendar at the end of each week to see how you've spent your time and also look ahead to the next week for planning purposes.

- **Your files** — Organize all paperwork that you receive or generate by handling it, filing it or throwing it away. Create your own filing system — whatever works best for you and your operational style.

  Tip 1: Establish a tickler file numbered one through 31 for each day of the month. Insert paperwork that needs to be handled on that particular day.
  Tip 2: Handle each piece of paper only once.
  Tip 3: Deal with all of your mail the day you receive it.

- **Your daily "To Do List"** — This is probably the most important tool for controlling your use of time. By addressing just 75 percent of the items on your list, you'll accomplish much more than your colleagues.

  Tip 1: Start with today's To Do List when compiling the one for tomorrow.
  Tip 2: Construct your To Do List by referring to your calendar and your tickler file.

Although these tips won't solve all of your time management problems, they should allow you more time to spend on your real job — working with your team.

6

COMMUNICATION

No Secrets

Dana Corporation operates by the motto, "There are no secrets at Dana." Employees are given full information about how the organization and their own work units are doing.

That policy includes how much profit is being made, the return on sales, the return on investment, etc. This information is communicated in the company newsletter, plant meetings, the chairman's regular letter to employees and one-on-one conferences.

Many supervisors and small business owners would be dubious about this policy. They imagine that when employees know a company is doing well, they will ask for more money. Dana found that if you don't let employees know about profits, they make up their own figures anyway and their speculations are more damaging to management's case than the truth. Surveys commonly indicate that the man-on-the-street thinks any company is retaining a profit of 35% to 50% of every dollar of sales, which is a vast exaggeration.

Some people hesitate to expose themselves to public question-and-answer sessions for fear that disgruntled employees will seek to embarrass them. Dana's experience is that no "cheap shot" questions have ever been posed to plant managers or the company chairman at such sessions. The questions employees ask are usually well thought-out, serious and express a concern they have about the company.

After the corporate staff visits a facility, members leave behind a poster with a tear-off sheet in the corner. Employees are invited to take a sheet, write their comments on it, fold it, insert it in a postage-paid mailer and send it to the chairman. He answers every single one, provided it is signed — and most are. He gets about 10 to 15 notes a week.

Finally, many supervisors and small business owners may be wary of plant or entire office meetings because of the apparent expense involved in shutting down the operation for them. Dana has found, to the contrary, that on meeting days production usually increases! The employees really appreciate the opportunity to be brought up-to-date on the events that affect them. They show it by making up the time taken out for the meeting by increasing their productivity the rest of the day.

Of course, many Dana plant managers feel somewhat shy or awkward about conducting such meetings. Therefore, the company chairman and president regularly visit the plants and conduct meetings to provide a role model for them and show that constructive meetings can be achieved.

Small business owners must learn to become comfortable leading those employee meetings. The more meetings you hold, the easier your role gets.

Communication Vehicles

While the previous section focused on Dana Corporation's use of all employee meetings as a form of communication, there are several other communication vehicles companies use to keep workers informed and morale high. As a small business owner, you may want to use some of these communication vehicles. As a supervisor, you need to understand their value and benefits.

- **Small group meetings** — These are often hosted by a senior-level manager from a large company or the owner of a small business. A representative cross-section of employees usually is invited to breakfast or lunch to ask questions, discuss issues, offer suggestions and provide feedback about the company. These meetings provide a good forum for the exchange of information.

- **Newsletters and magazines** — These publications usually are distributed on a weekly, bi-weekly or monthly basis to all company employees. They may contain news about the company, its industry or competitors — any information that employees should know and care about. In addition, these publications often feature interesting stories about employees' accomplishments both on and off the job, employee letters, birthdays and service anniversaries. Sometimes newsletters and magazines are sent to employees' homes so family members also learn the latest company news.

- **Bulletins** — When urgent company news occurs, bulletins or brief news flashes can be written on company letterhead and distributed quickly to each employee or department. In some instances, the company CEO or small business owner may want to inform employees of the news in a personal letter.

- **Electronic mail** — In a computerized office environment electronic mail, or e-mail as it's often called, is being used more and more to keep employees informed. Information often included in newsletters and bulletins can be distributed easily and efficiently through e-mail. However, there is one major drawback for using e-mail for all employee information. Some company employees may not have access to it on a regular basis.

- **Videotapes** — Because of the costs associated with producing videotapes, most companies use them for specific and/or special purposes: introducing a new product or service, employee training or orientation, documenting an event or sending recorded messages from the CEO or small business owner to remote locations.

Communication: It's Also Appearance

Witnessing

A key role for supervisors and small business owners is "witnessing," according to Philip Crosby, author of *Running Things: The Art of Making Things Happen*. Supervisors should be aware that their people are looking to them for a reading on how things are going.

For example, in 1982, Crosby's own company was going through a recession. Things were very tough and it was touch-and-go as to whether the company would survive.

As he went around the company, Crosby could see that people were observing him. So he went around smiling and offering encouragement.

Had he looked perpetually disheartened, the company might have gone under. With such an example, any employee with sense would start looking for another job.

Crosby believes leaders set the tone for their teams and so they must be aware of "witnessing" for the good of the organization and themselves.

A Different Kind of Communication

Working to Survive

For many businesses, especially those in highly competitive markets, survival cannot be taken for granted. Supervisors and small business owners know that only maximum efficiency and effort on everyone's part will enable the company to survive. But how can they convey that same sense of urgency to their employees without frightening or discouraging them?

Harwood Cochran, chairman of Overnite Transportation Co., uses an effective method. *Forbes* magazine reports that every time a competitor goes bankrupt, Cochran puts the failed trucker's logo up on his red brick wall underneath a sign that reads, "Deregulation done 'em in." He has mounted 47 company logos, with room for plenty more.

"I want my employees to know that we're not guaranteed to be here," Cochran explains. His employees have cooperated with OTC's economy measures and, as a result, Cochran's business is profitable in an industry wracked with closings and red ink.

If you need to alert employees to stressful conditions in your industry, keep them vividly aware of competitors, problems and they'll draw the needed inferences about your firm.

How to Communicate More Powerfully

The Five-Step Formula for Clear Work Instructions

1. *Be friendly.* Instructions given in a friendly way are more likely to be met with friendly and willing cooperation.

2. *Keep it simple.* Your instructions should be clear and concise. Make sure you have organized your thoughts and have a clear idea of the outcome you want.

3. *Not just what, but why.* Explain not just what is going to be done, but why the action is being taken.

4. *Get feedback.* Ask employees if they have any questions or suggestions. Ask them to tell you what they are going to do. Do not ask them if they understand.

5. *Follow up.* Monitor the activity of your employees to see if instructions are being followed. Even better, ask them to report their progress periodically.

Giving Directions

Beverly Potter, management consultant, suggests using the DAD system when giving orders. DAD stands for *Describe*, *Ask for clarification* and *Direct*.

- *Describe* the problem situation objectively, specifically, simply and without accusations to the employee. ("Jim, your district is lagging behind the others in sales. We need at least a 10 percent increase in the next six months.")

- *Ask* the employee how he or she feels about the situation and for suggestions. This clarifies the problem and gives you added perspective. ("What's your view of the sales problem? How might we best achieve that goal?")

- *Direct* the employee in simple, concrete terms, considering his or her suggestions when possible. Ask for further clarification if you think the directive might be misunderstood. ("I agree that a promotional campaign should be launched. Do you foresee any obstacles to doing that?")

The DAD system is especially appropriate with an employee whose opinion is important and whose actions must be directed.

Key Points for Improving Oral Communication

Here are some helpful hints for one-on-one conversations.

1. Decide in advance the outcome you want from the conversation.

2. Take a minute to organize your thoughts before you begin. It may help if you jot down some key points. In most situations there is absolutely nothing wrong with referring to your notes. It can even strengthen the impression you make.

3. Listen to what the other party is saying — *really listen*. Don't think about what you are going to say next.

4. Solicit feedback from friends about your one-on-one oral skills. Be prepared to hear some criticism.

5. Tape record yourself. You might be amazed at some sloppy speech habits you are unaware of. Uhs, ands and you knows are the most common.

Communicating in Letters, Memos and Reports

Follow these guidelines in your written communication.

1. Make an outline of your thoughts, including an open, middle and

close. Look particularly at the organization of your material. Do you cover each point before moving on? Do your thoughts flow logically? Do you make a smooth transition between major points?

2. Get feedback on your written skills. Again, don't take the criticism personally.

3. Don't avoid writing. You can only get better at what you practice.

4. Analyze material you read. Whether it's a well-written memo or a magazine article that you like, examine what made the material clear, concise and interesting to read.

However you choose to communicate, it's another important step toward building a strong work team and a successful business.

Index